Chapter 1

DAHLIA

I0683226

I've tried to meditate. My father always said it would calm me down, quell my deviant nature and even make me happy, but it was difficult. My mind would skip from one thought to the next, trying desperately to keep busy, like a slave working harder and faster each day, no matter how filthy or demeaning the task, anything to keep the mind off his reality. Mania, or attention deficit disorder, as some call it, is actually a saving grace to those of us who cannot bear to do nothing. The nothing forces us to be with ourselves, with our mistakes, our insecurities, our failures; it forces us to be victims—and it's painful. It is so much easier to complete tasks and make lists and forge revolutions, and so I did. I forged a revolution and created a new world—my reward, a century of nothing. There, alone in the darkness, thinking of nothing, like a candle burning bright in a windowless cell, I was alive in there. I had stories to tell, love to give, and rage. I had mostly rage. But no one could see it. No one could see me.

I suppose that I looked like a lunatic, talking to myself—one minute I was calm, and the next I was flushed with lust or anger. I'm sure you've seen them, the crazies, walking down the street, in the emergency room, in a movie, or at the very least conjured up in your own imagination. That was me, Dahlia, the crazy woman. After a decade of nothing, I tried to imagine what the people beyond the cold metal of my prison were like, what they felt. It began with a jolt of panic or surge of lust. For a few seconds at a time, I could tune into their thoughts and experience their fears and their joys. Of course, it's much easier to do face to face, but endless time and practice gave me the strength to push past the average skill level of my kind, the manic, and become excellent—even superior.

At first, I could only imagine beyond the tiny box or closet I was kept in, then to the adjacent room, then to the hallway or common living space, then to the street outside or the neighbor's house, until finally an entire community of feelings and thoughts buzzed in my head. I became addicted to it. Like diving off a cliff into the water, it was all at once terrifying and exhilarating. It lasted for only moments at a time, but each time was more satisfying than the next. I couldn't stop. For generations, I imagined the consciousness of those around me. I felt the excitement of little Malik when he snuck out of his house, the butterflies in Sarrah's stomach when she kissed her boyfriend, the blind drunken rage of Tomas as he sat alone on the floor, a neighbor's jealousy over land, and even the lust Asem felt for his cousin. Like countless others, Malik, Sarrah, Tomas, and Asem have come and gone. I miss being able to see with them, touch with them, smell with them, be them.

Sometimes I would be taken places, and I could feel the warmth of the sun or the rough sweat-soaked sand as it got caught in the links of my chain. It was only ever for a day or two, a week at most, and then I went back into a box, back into the darkness—until, of course, Liana. I always thought she could feel me, like her mother did, but I was never certain. I will always regret how I affected her mother. She wasn't strong enough and, I should have felt that. Maybe I did. The want for freedom is difficult to shake. But her daughter, she was different-—stronger, smarter, impulsive, and trusting to a fault—just like me. If she only knew the things I would show her, she might have worn me sooner. But she didn't. I don't know what made her take me that night, but then and every night after, I helped her see my thoughts, my mistakes, my secrets, my strengths, and, finally, my purpose: to grant her wishes.

Chapter *2*

LIANA

She stood in front of a dressing room door. This room was separate from the others. Presumably someone special must occupy it, but there was no star on the door, not even a lock. Liana glanced down at her simple, elegant red summer dress; at least she thought it was elegant—*would he?* She followed it down across her hips until she reached my prison, the gold ankle bracelet with the flawed but still impenetrable locket charm that sparkled above her foot. I was a part of her now, if only by extension, and could feel her thoughts—*was the ankle bracelet too much? Would he disapprove or expect more?* Liana's eyes fell upon the door once more; she knocked and then opened it.

Inside she found dozens of old promotional posters for various magic and illusionist performances. The same person appeared in all of them, at first a four-year-old boy with the trademark top hat, bow tie, and magic wand. As Liana followed the posters across the room, one by one the venues got bigger, and the man at the center of it all got grander. Headlines read: "Phenomenon, Four-Year-Old

Magician," "Jamison Sets the Bar for Illusionists Everywhere," "Jamison Makes the White House Disappear." Then the posters began to lose their luster, their sense of grandeur. Evidence of his decline surrounded the room: old black-and-white photos turned yellow, drawers and cabinets missed handles, dusty awards scattered among other, once meaningful trinkets. And just like the posters, in the middle of the room perched an old, stoic man: Jamison the Great. He sat wearing an over-the-top genie costume. Any other man would've looked like a washed-up mascot to some Middle Eastern sports franchise, but not Jamison. His garments became a part of him and, once shed, would take their rightful place among his proud display of previously worn costumes and previous identities. Jamison was, as they say, old-school—a reminder of the gravitas one could have before the age of social media and constant surveillance. He spotted Liana's reflection in his mirror and lit up.

"Hi, honey!" he said.

"Hi, Daddy," Liana replied.

Their embrace was genuine, not formal or forced. Jamison clung to her like a good-luck charm until his eyes fell upon the sparkle just above Liana's foot. She knew he saw it; she could tell by the empty space that wedged its way in between their bodies, only a millimeter or so, but still it was there. The ankle bracelet continued to sparkle up at him, almost as if it were taunting him, daring him to react—*and I was.*

"What are you doing back here?" asked Jamison, as he pulled away from her.

"Oh, I just thought I'd come back to say—"

"Don't say it."

"Break a leg."

They smiled at each other for a moment, and in that moment, a dozen silent conversations played themselves out in each of their minds, but before they could speak, before they could reconcile their feelings, there was another knock at the door.

"Come in," said Jamison.

The door opened to reveal another elder man. This one was frail and hunched over with sweat pouring down his forehead until it got stuck in a pool building up above his large bushy eyebrows, almost like a dam holding back a river. An unexpected sneeze sent the sweat flying through the air until it landed on a scuffed wooden chair. Despite his unappealing appearance, he seemed harmless.

"Hi, Stefan," said Jamison.

"Hi, Jamison," Stefan replied. "Are you ready for your harness?"

"Yes."

Stefan peeked fondly at Liana as he approached Jamison with a large black harness.

"Oh, I'm sorry," said Jamison, "How rude of me. This is my daughter, Liana. Liana, this is one of my crew members, Stefan."

It was strange that she had never seen him before; she had been to a few of the rehearsals.

"Pleasure to meet you," said Stefan.

"Likewise," she said.

But she didn't mean it. I could feel the temperature in her body become cooler. Somehow, for some reason, it wasn't a pleasure meeting him. In fact, she had never felt so much distaste for another person in her life. Part mystified and part mortified by her reaction, Liana tried to remain as benign as possible, for she didn't want to start trouble right before opening night. She watched silently as Stefan began to attach the large black harness to Jamison's back and undercarriage. As he bent over, Liana noticed a tattoo of black script across the back of Stefan's neck. He spotted her looking at it.

"Don't worry, miss. We've rehearsed this a thousand times," said Stefan.

"Yes, I know," said Liana.

"Your father is the greatest magician in the world. You have nothing to worry about."

Their eyes met again for a second, and in that second, Liana felt a slight sting in her left eye—*I felt it, too.* She blinked and turned her head away from Jamison so he wouldn't see her reaction.

"I better go find my seat," she said.

"Thank you for coming back to see me, sweetheart," said Jamison.

"Sure, Dad. I'll see you after the show."

As she opened the door to the dressing room, Stefan peered at her once more.

"It was nice meeting you," he said.

Liana forced a smile then exited.

Hidden behind a heavy red curtain, she walked like an unwelcome guest among performers dressed in vague genie-like costumes doing various warm-up exercises. Of course, she was welcome, at least on the surface. Whether they truly liked her would remain a mystery, as none would dare rebuke the daughter of their boss. Still, Liana smiled politely and continued across the stage through a door to the makeup area. Her reflection followed her across the room through a series of mirrors surrounded by bright lights. Liana's ankle bracelet sparkled against her olive skin. Again, she wondered, did he like what she was wearing? Was her hair okay? As six images of her bounced off the multiple mirrors lined up against the wall, six pairs of hands ran themselves through the front, back, and sides of her black hair. It was too much. She looked like the homecoming queen, not the daughter of a great illusionist. But as much as she tried to deny it, it wasn't her hair, her makeup, or even her dress that was too much; it was the sparkle of my home, the locket on the golden ankle bracelet—a gift from Jamison to Liana's mother. The one tangible reminder of what she was like before it started happening, before she went away. Liana's mother wore that ankle bracelet from the day Jamison gave it to her, and every day after. It was a part of her, the one part that stayed constant. And now, Liana wore it, on the opening night of her father's most important performance in a decade. It was a choice that Liana had struggled with for weeks. Time after time, the decision to wear the ankle bracelet almost always came to a no, but there was something about this day, something that drew her to it, *to me*. A psychologist might say it was her subconscious lashing out, looking for excitement, looking for a risk—looking to sabotage her father. And yet, I sensed that he mattered more to her than any other man, or boy, could.

Liana left the makeup room and came face to face with a large white horse. She wasn't stunned or surprised but just reached out her hand and said, "Hi, Taffy."

The horse's handler, just a few feet behind them, gently coaxed the horse toward Liana, and she reached out to give him a good scratch behind the ears. She and Taffy, the horse, had come to know each other quite well during the few rehearsals she chaperoned. Taffy was the most dangerous part of the show, and she couldn't bear the thought of her father in an accident. And although she recognized her own self-inflicted anticipation of disaster, Jamison never once had an accident when she was around.

"Okay, Taffy," she began, "you ready to make history?" She nudged the handler with her elbow. "He's ready, right?"

"Don't worry. We've rehearsed this about a thousand times," he said.

"Yes, I know."

"He'll be fine, I promise."

Feeling reassured, Liana left them with a smile on her face. And as she rounded the corner, Taffy in turn reassured his handler by urinating on the stage floor.

Liana finally emerged from the bowels of the stage and found her plush red seat located in the center mezzanine section of a ninety-year-old majestic theater. Its art deco features were a perfect match for the anticipated performance, a combination of both modern and ancient influences. The house lights went down, and the heavy red curtain rose to reveal a single male performer dressed in a baggy Middle Eastern garment. Surrounding him were various campy props: large sabers and golden daggers adorned with fake jewels; statues of top-heavy men with dark goatees, some of them with long ponytails, some topless, others in tightly fitted vests. Most of their bottom halves were images of smoke or fog, as if the sculptor became tired or simply didn't know how to fashion a pair of legs in baggy pants with elf shoes out of wood or stone. The man on stage looked defeated. Then, from the darkness of this commercialized world of genie folklore, appeared a simple wooden door.

The man approached the door cautiously, first touching it, then feeling it, and finally listening to it. A single note was heard from the darkness, circulating among the many arcs and pockets of space built into the theater. The note hung in the air until it transformed into Arabic lyrics, elegantly sung by an unseen force. Smoke poured over the edge of the stage. The door opened to reveal a soft glow of light. The man's eyes widened with excitement. Liana felt it, too. It was like finding a new chapter from a tired, emasculated tale that had once brought a sense of wonder and fear to its readers. The man grabbed a nearby sword and walked through the door.

Suddenly, the stage transformed into a world of passion with warm colors and seductive sounds. Four dancers dressed in revealing, black, genie-like costumes, two male and two female, spun down like yo-yos from the ceiling on red fabric. Just before landing on the stage below, the red fabric combusted and disappeared like flash paper. The dancers pulsed in and out of the fog trying to touch each other. With every close encounter, they were propelled in opposite directions as if they were similar charges of giant human magnets.

Sand fell in four streams from the ceiling into four separate baskets spaced out randomly onstage. Beneath the fog rose a hollow glass mold of Jamison. It was spectacular, just as Jamison was. The four dancers, one by one, grabbed a basket, now filled with sand, and poured it into the glass mold. As the sand reached the top, the Middle Eastern man in baggy clothes emerged from the darkness. Sword still in hand, he struck the glass mold. It shattered, sending the sand onto the floor to reveal the real Jamison.

The audience cheered! Liana proudly clapped. Jamison graciously bowed to the audience. His hands rose up, and with them, four cobra snakes from the baskets onstage. Fangs exposed, the snakes continued to rise until suspended in midair. The dancers moved under and around them in a choreographed routine. Again, applause filled the room.

The lights and sound made a drastic shift. As the room turned from passionate red to a cool blue and gray, Liana, now fully vested in what was happening in front of her, became cold. In fact, for a moment, she could swear she saw her breath. A feeling of anticipation, with accompanying sounds from the orchestra, filled the room. The dancers exited the stage, with snakes in hand, leaving Jamison alone. He took off his cloak and passed it through the air to reveal the white horse, Taffy. The audience cooed with approval as Jamison expertly mounted the horse. The anxious dulcet tones gained momentum and rattled through the pockets of the theater. Taffy suddenly reared and jumped into the air but didn't come back down. Both Jamison and Taffy floated in the air like a piece of pineapple stuck in a Jell-O mold. The audience cheered!

In the midst of the excitement, Liana noticed a small flash from behind the stage. Taffy reared up, throwing Jamison off his back. Liana stood up. The crowd gasped with concern. Jamison swung back and forth on his harness until it snapped, swinging him upside down. Taffy was promptly lowered to the stage and immediately defecated.

"Help! Somebody help me!" said Jamison.

He swung back and forth like a misshapen pendulum on an old grandfather clock. Laughter began to slowly mix in with the gasps of horror from the audience.

"Stop it!" said Liana. "Somebody help him. What are you all doing?"

The laughter grew into an uproarious white noise.

"Stop it!"

Chapter 3

THE FIRST DREAM

I stood before a single tree in a mountain valley. A rope, dangling from one of its branches, held a man upside down. He was beaten and bruised, wearing only filthy rags around his pelvic region. A motley crew of dark, exotic-looking men and women surrounded him. Some of them were topless, others had odd markings across their bodies, and all were scantily clad. One of the men spit fire at the torso of the hanging man. He screamed then writhed in pain. Blisters began to form around his belly button. The crowd laughed.

"Stop it! Leave him alone!" I said, commanding the peasant riffraff. They immediately backed away, as if confronted by an angry tiger. I rushed toward the hanging man.

"I'm so sorry, Alexander."

He looked up into my eyes, one of them blue and the other green. My long dark hair dragged across the bloody gashes on his face as I tried to set him upright. His shoulder rested on mine, upside down, like interlocking pieces of a puzzle. His blood started to flow down across my neck and into the valley of my chest. A sudden gust of wind pushed back my long, sand–

colored cloak to reveal a white, scarf-like garment that traveled down my body in a snake-like fashion.

"You're a long way from home, my dear," muttered an elder man hidden among the deviant crowd.

I looked up. A faceless figure emerged from the pack, revealing only a dark cloak and a tattoo of script on the back of his neck.

"Leave us," he commanded.

The ruffians scattered into the mountain caves. I knew the faceless figure well and wished that he would remain so, as the sight of him pushed me only further into the dark.

"Let him go," I said.

"You know I cannot. The laws will not allow it," he replied.

I looked into the swollen flesh around Alexander's eyes. If only I could somehow take his place, or suffer for him; even binding would be better than this—better than the guilt I felt.

"This is my fault. I brought him here."

The elder man feigned concern "I'm sorry. You know I—"

"I'll do it."

"What?"

He knew what I was referring to. All this time, he thought the lives of my own kind would be his leverage, but instead, it would be the life of a human, this human.

"If you let him go, I'll marry you."

The elder man began to walk away. These words, the same words I dared not to utter for years, came too easily from my lips. This insult bred saliva in his mouth, and in return, he spat on Alexander's face.

"Stop it! Release him and you can have me," I said, "just as our fathers wanted. Then there can still be a truce between us."

The elder man looked at me and the way I held Alexander, the way I plunged myself into his peasant filth without any regard for my own well-being or my own kind.

"And if you're playing me for a fool?" he said.

"I'm not."

I was indeed playing him for a fool and would continue to in perpetuity. Fools, however, believe diplomacy and compromise begin and end with their own self-interests, and as such, I would have to give him something, if not myself, something just as valuable and coveted.

"I do not believe you," he whispered.

He waved his hand, and the rope holding Alexander grew like a vine around his neck.

"No!" I said.

Although I tried, I could no longer find reason; I could no longer calculate my next action. The adult in me had been stifled by the gasps for breath, the gushing blood and swollen eyes that hung before me. I needed to save him; I needed to do it now.

"I'll give you my name!"

16

Chapter 4

PURPLE ROOM

Liana's torso catapulted up from her bed like a sprung rattrap. Her forehead was damp with sweat, her hair pulled back in a ponytail, and I was still wrapped around her ankle. My influence over Liana's dreams came easier than I expected, and although there was more to reveal, I couldn't show her too much all at once—a mistake I made with her mother. The bedroom, bathed in a soft lavender color with white accents, seemed to immediately calm her down, as if being wrapped in a soft, warm blanket. Beside her sat a large glass bowl filled with loose change and a glass of water half full. Liana looked up at the reflection of herself in a vanity mirror directly across from her, took a deep breath, and opened her covers. They were a bright yellow, an appropriate match for the rest of the room; however, they suggested a kind of dissonance from their surroundings. Liana often felt this way. As a person's clothes become an extension of themselves, their persona, so did Liana's bedcovers when she lay to sleep. She fit in to her environment just fine but, at the same time, didn't quite belong.

Dressed in a paint-stained, dark blue T-shirt and white, cutoff sweatpants, Liana wiped her brow and stepped into a flimsy pair of flip-flops. I could hear them snap against her heels as she stepped out of her room and down a flight of stairs. At the bottom, she spotted her father sitting at the kitchen table reading the paper. Although his back was to her, she could feel the expression on his face, an expression of deep disappointment.

"Good morning, Daddy," said Liana.

She walked over to the kitchen counter, flip-flops snapping with each stride, and poured two cups of coffee.

"The broken harness wasn't the only folly in Jamison's performance," read Jamison. *"His recycled tricks and overused theatrics were barely a suggestion of the great magician we once knew. We respect what he's done for illusionists in the past, but he simply does not belong on the stage anymore."* Liana took the paper out of his hands and replaced it with a cup of coffee.

"Don't pay any attention to this, Dad. It was an accident. Accidents happen."

"Not to me," he said, taking the coffee.

And he was right, they never happened, at least when she was around.

"It wasn't your fault," said Liana.

Jamison lifted his coffee to take a drink, and his hand began to uncharacteristically shake.

"Daddy, are you okay?"

"I'm fine, I just can't..."

He struggled with the cup of coffee like trying to complete the last rep in a series of barbell curls. Liana glanced up at a large brass serving plate hanging in a decorative fashion on the wall across from Jamison. She watched the reflection of his hand shaking as the cup hovered below his mouth. She examined more closely and saw the reflection of a third hand holding down Jamison's. Liana blinked, and the third hand was gone. Jamison's hand stopped trembling and swung up to his mouth, as if breaking free from a wad of tar. A drop of coffee broke free from the cup and landed under his nose.

"Dad, did you see that?" said Liana.

Jamison gestured for a napkin.

"See what?" he said, wiping his nose.

Liana paused for a moment and wondered whether all the years of witnessing illusions were starting to affect her reality.

"Nothing," she said as she handed him a napkin.

Jamison set his coffee down and began to clean himself up.

Something in his face had changed. It was as if he lost something that he only moments ago held in his unbreakable grasp. I wanted to know. I wanted to feel what he felt.

"There was nothing I could do about the harness," he said.

Liana smiled, but instead of evoking a feeling of acceptance, it conjured up a feeling of resentment. He didn't like to be placated; no one does. He wasn't ready for retirement, for surrender. He had held on this long and wasn't going to let go.

"Like I said before, accidents happen," Liana said. "Isn't that what you always told Mom?"

Jamison's eyes fell upon the ankle bracelet—*on me*. It was a strange look, one of longing and at the same time surrender. That same feeling he had only moments ago denounced, he suddenly accepted without struggle or hesitation. *Was the defiant child inside of him so instantly brought to his knees by a single thought of Liana's mother?*

"Yes, it is," he said. "If only there was a rehearsal for life."

Liana smiled and lowered her head. I knew she wanted to apologize, to acknowledge her mistake, but she couldn't. She longed for her mother, too, at least the version of her before it started happening, and she had every right to wear the ankle bracelet.

Jamison also knew what she was thinking, but he couldn't bring himself to apologize, either; it was his duty to protect his daughter from harm, even if it was from her own mother, even if it was from just a thought. He set his napkin down and began to stand. Halfway up, he got stuck.

"Are you okay?" said Liana.

"I'm fine. Just a little stiff from the fall."

Liana looked over at his reflection in the brass plate. This time, she saw the silhouette of a young man holding Jamison down at the shoulders.

"Stop it!" she said.

The silhouette vanished, and Jamison became erect.

"Dad, did you see that?" said Liana.

"I know. I straightened right up."

"No, in the plate, there was a…"

Liana scanned the kitchen. Everything was in its place. As mismatched as those things were: an olive green stove and oven next to a stainless-steel refrigerator; an auburn, rustic laminate countertop met by a black-and-white tile backsplash; and a detached, stand-alone dishwasher masquerading as a kitchen island. As out of sync as everything was, it was somehow in sync. Again, Liana thought her mind was playing tricks on her.

"Nothing, never mind."

Chapter 5

AN INCIDENT

Liana walked down a narrow sidewalk, passing a large poster of her school mascot, a red Griffin. It looked up at its owner, a large high school, half 1920s-era ornate architecture and half Modern Museum of Art. This time-honored institution was literally being consumed by a modern expansion, made to make room for the increase in population. It was a monument to the invasion of the digital age.

Liana's friend, Rachel, walked next to her in the latest bohemian garb, made acceptable to her fellow private school elit only by her mainstream hairstyle and status-affirming jewelry. dense early morning fog hovered above them.

"I can't believe you're blowing off the party tonight home with your dad," said Rachel.

"He's getting older, Rachel. This morning he I standing, and his hand was shaking."

"Okay, but he can take care of himself. H mother, didn't he?"

Liana nodded. It was true. He did take care of her mother. And one could argue, if he could take care of her, he could handle anything. But still, he had never had an accident before now, before the ankle bracelet.

They turned the corner and entered the high school through a heavy wooden door. Several other students showcased the usual high-school shenanigans, hipsters skateboarded in the hall, and the BPs (beautiful people) texted as they sauntered by.

"So does that mean you're coming?" said Rachel.

"No, my dad just fell off a horse; I don't want him to be alone."

Rachel's face fell like a Salvador Dalí painting. Liana could tell she had had enough. This wasn't the first party, or even the first social event, that Liana had blown off. It was becoming a habit.

"Okay," said Rachel, "when are you going to forgive him?"

"Never," answered Liana without missing a beat.

"Come on, Liana, I'm sorry that your two-year high-school boyfriend cheated on you for six months while the whole school talked about it behind your back, but you need to move on."

A bright red dot, dancing like an over-caffeinated flea, appeared on Rachel's chest.

"I have moved on," said Liana.

"Knock it off, loser!" said Rachel as she swung her bag at a laser pointer–wielding classmate behind Liana, "Sorry, Liana."

"Yeah, I know you're sorry, everyone's sorry."

They both knew that wasn't what Rachel meant, but neither acknowledged it. It was true. Everyone had kept a horrible secret from her, even Rachel. And why? What was the point? To occupy their boring, mundane heads with something entertaining? God forbid they engage in something meaningful.

"At least my dad doesn't keep secrets from me," said Liana as she walked away.

Rachel stood for a moment and let her go. She may be hardheaded and obnoxious, but she could still pick up social cues, at least until she became bored with them.

"You can't let one stupid guy ruin your life forever!"

A faint smoke passed by her, almost like it was following Liana.

Rachel wrinkled her nose. "Hey, there's no smoking in here! This is a smoke-free zone!"

Rachel coughed and then darted after Liana into a nearby classroom. She pulled a computer tablet out of her bag and sat at a desk next to Liana. About forty other students sat at desks around them, all equidistant from each other. Each student was equipped with a computer tablet or small notebook computer. In keeping with the modern style of paperless education, the room was armed with digital enhancements. The walls, however, remain aged with cracks and water damage in the corners. This damage gave the room character, only a little, though, as the digital enhancements seemed to force the damaged exterior to assimilate, like a new virus growing stronger inside a dilapidated body.

An old professor entered the room. With his skin as damaged as the walls, and his character as distinguished and stoic, he faced his students with certainty. They responded to his presence in the usual way, half attentive, half daydreaming, except for one, the jerk from the laser pointer–incident prior. He sat in the back of the classroom feverishly typing on his computer.

"Good morning, class," said the professor. "Today, we're going to be continuing our discussion of the djinn, or as you more commonly refer to them, genies."

As the students' faces lit up from their computer screens, the jerk continued typing in the back.

"In Arabic, the term *djinn* literally means 'invisibility' or 'concealment,'" said the professor. "That is why we cannot see them. Unless of course they want to be seen, but they never do."

The jerk glanced over at Liana then hit the Enter key on his computer.

"Please touch the images icon on your history application," said the professor as he swiped across his own computer tablet.

As he touched an icon, the large screen at the front of the room lit up, and a GIF of Jamison from his accident the night before began to play on repeat: Jamison swung upside-down over a pile of horse feces, back and forth, back and forth, back and forth. The students began to laugh. Liana stared at the video in disbelief.

"Ladies and gentlemen, I expect you to take my class seriously," said the professor. "This is not a playground!"

He deleted the video from the screen as the students continued to snicker. Rachel tried to contain a smile.

"It's not funny!" said Liana as she got up and stormed out of the classroom.

"Liana, I'm sorry," said Rachel. "Wait! I didn't mean to laugh."

She followed Liana out of the classroom and down an empty hallway until they rounded a corner and stopped at the top of a staircase.

"Don't you think this is hard enough for me?!" said Liana.

"I know. I'm sorry!"

A strange thick fog began to circle and rise up her legs.

"You're supposed to be my friend!"

"I am your friend."

"No, you're not!" screamed Liana, and the fog knocked Rachel off her feet and down the staircase.

Chapter 6

DR. RATTNER

Liana sat in a plush green office. Her chair, covered in mahogany leather, stood in the center of the room facing another chair. The hardwood floors hid under a large tasseled rug decorated in green and brown geometric patterns. It was obvious the rug came first, before the green paint on the walls, before the various odd gentlemen framed by wood and silver hanging on the wall. They were all so serious, looking down on her, as if in judgment of the lesser than. Men like that didn't exist anymore, not in the twenty-first century. And if they had dared to presume to be above the less educated or less wealthy, an Internet troll would almost certainly post a compromising video or photo of them, exposing their vices, one like the GIF of her father in her classroom.

As she looked at the person sitting across from her, Liana thought about how strange it was that all these framed men of judgment fell in line behind a woman, the woman sitting across from her, Dr. Joyce Rattner. Her suit matched the room perfectly, a subtle green accented by her dark brown hair. She definitely fit in and was not at all like Liana.

It was clear that was not their first meeting. They had long passed the phase of trying to find common ground or gain admiration and approval. It was time to get down to business, to make a decision—a decision that would affect the rest of Liana's life, her father's life, and all of those around her.

"I think it's time to start you on some medication," said Dr. Rattner.

Liana looked away.

Dr. Rattner leaned into her "I know. Your mother didn't want to take it, either."

"I'm fine," said Liana.

"Liana, you just told me that you've been seeing weird reflections, disembodied hands, mysterious fog—"

"It's just stress."

"So you did push that girl down the stairs?"

"No, I didn't."

Dr. Rattner rested back in her chair. "Schizophrenia can be a very dangerous condition. Your mother found that out the hard way."

Liana turned her head, searching for comfort from one of those odd men on the wall staring back at her.

"I know it seems real, but these things you're seeing are just in your mind. This disease is hereditary. It's not your fault, but we need to start you on medicine now, before it gets worse."

"I said I'm fine," said Liana. "I'm just worried about my dad. He's been through a lot, especially with Mom."

"Yes, he has. He's been through a lot. Do you want to see him suffer all over again?"

Liana was offended. Her cheeks became flushed and her ears hot. She was embarrassed and sad—sad that she couldn't retreat back to blissful ignorance. She tried to pretend that the choice to wear her mother's ankle bracelet on Jamison's opening night was hers, but the truth is, it wasn't. She couldn't control herself then, and she might not be able to in the future.

"Do you want to see your father suffer?"

"No."

Dr. Rattner smiled. She didn't seem happy, though; it was something else. Her shoulders dropped and her eyebrows were released from the hold of her creased forehead muscles. She acted more relieved than she did triumphant, like she just got out of a speeding ticket or passed a pop quiz. She grabbed a pen, calmly took out a pad of prescription paper, and wrote the word *lithium*.

Just outside the office, a young female secretary sat behind a modern desk surrounded by a glass partition. She smiled as Liana walked by her and toward the exit. There, like a bouncer at the latest nightclub, stood a young man obstructing the doorway. As his back was toward Liana, she could not make out his face.

"Excuse me," she said.

He didn't move. His short dark hair and olive skin seamlessly faded into his earthy leather clothing, haphazardly sewn together by jagged strings of what looked like blonde human hair. Liana followed the threading of the hair across the garment over his chest, and it suddenly started moving, as if swimming the breaststroke through a pool of faded latex. After just surrendering the notion that her basic impulses had any validity or base in reality, Liana wasn't surprised or shocked, and simply tried again.

"Excuse me. I need to get out."

Still, he did nothing. Liana looked around the room, searching for anything that might cue her next move.

"Can I help you, miss?" asked the secretary.

"Yes, this man won't get out of my way."

"What man?"

Liana looked back at the doorway, and he was gone. Dr. Rattner was right. The hallucinations were beginning to affect her life and the lives of those around her and would certainly be too much for her already-ailing father.

"Never mind," she said. "I was just talking to myself."

On the way home, Liana drove with extreme caution: hands at

ten and two, headlights on, music off. The needle never strayed more than a millimeter or two from the line marked "30" on her speedometer. If the meeting with Dr. Rattner was meant to relieve her anxiety, it had almost certainly failed. Now, blinded by the anticipation of phantom people or things, Liana half expected a pair of displaced hippos to appear having tea on the hood of her car. Too nervous to take her eyes off the road for even a second, she abandoned the thought of reaching for the air conditioning and, consequently, began to perspire.

Having safely arrived home, Liana sat on her bright yellow bed, staring out at the soft purple walls around her. She looked at a bottle of medicine in her hand, clearly marked "Lithium." Liana suddenly got up, tore off her bright yellow sheets, and replaced them with a lavender set. Taking pride in her decision, she made the bed with military precision, and even bounced a quarter off the bed, taken from her bowl of loose change. In a final farewell to her previous life, Liana sat quietly on her bed, took a small pill from the bottle of medicine, and accepted it with a glass of water.

Chapter 7

A BIRD AND A FISH

A brush of color, first dark purple, then orange, and finally a bright yellow, spilled across the sky until it was met by the sea, far off in the distance. The horizon, an intangible barrier that was both everywhere and nowhere, split the two worlds, one of brilliance and the other of vast darkness, the sky and ocean. These two worlds existed side by side, creating a beautiful landscape: a landscape that was flawless but for one towering cliff. This cliff tore into the sky and ocean like a knife through a painting. Its jagged edges carved a third world into the landscape, a world that was new, disruptive, and taboo. The pioneers of this world, Alexander, now dressed in eighteenth-century colonial garb, and I, in a stark white dress, sat on a blanket atop the cliff, hand in hand, ready to risk anything and everything for our lives together.

"Your home is beautiful," said Alexander, as he leaned in to kiss me.

"Thank you."

I looked down at our joined hands. Our banter was sweet and sincere but also redundant. These words had been spoken already, and no amount of gratitude or commitment could prevent what was to come.

"Are you going to tell him tonight?" said Alexander.

I raised my head to expose a single tear on my cheek.

"I don't know. I don't think he's ready."

"He's going to find out sooner or later."

"I know. I just don't want to ruin this."

Alexander wiped the tear off my face. I must've looked so sad, so defeated, for I could feel his thoughts ringing in my head like a desperate auctioneer. Was this all too much for her? Did she regret saving me? Was I asking too much or not sacrificing enough? Maybe I wasn't ready, or maybe she wasn't ready. *And then he thought about what life would be like without me, without knowing I ever existed. We would both be safe, content enough, and the two worlds in that beautiful landscape would remain untouched, untorn. But then we would never know that fabled feeling of love, true love. As cliché as that sounded in my head, I could still remember how my limbs went numb the first time we touched. How else would one describe it? Love. A man of science would tell you that it's simple brain chemistry, nothing more, nothing magical. If pheromones and symmetry had no effect and did not prompt the release of corticosteroids in the body, there would be no feeling of love or euphoria, and consequently no life. What would the world be like then? A world with loveless marriages and empty touches. It sounded terrible.*

"Nothing can ruin this," he said. "You can't take away what we've been given."

I looked over at him, at his monochromatic eyes, and wondered what our children might look like. This feeling, this hope for the future, made me dizzy. My arms went numb, and I felt lighter than air.

"I feel it again!"

We embraced and kissed softly. If love were a simple chemical reaction in the brain designed to help a species survive, then how could it be happening to us? Surely a bird could never love a fish. There would be no point, no logical conclusion, no species to propagate. And yet, it had happened. Our two worlds had come together. And if it had all ended at that moment, with no logical conclusion, it would have been worth it, because that was true love.

That pointed cliff tearing into our landscape was no longer an intruder but rather another layer of beauty. And up above it, a genie and a human rose up on a blanket and floated together toward the sunset.

Chapter **8**

TAFFI

Liana again sprang up from her newly congruous bed, this time in the dead of night. She, too, suddenly felt dizzy and fell back against her headboard. *Had I revealed too much this time, or was the medication making her sick?* Half expecting to be floating in midair on her mattress, Liana leaned over the bed to confirm its foothold on the ground. The bed was, indeed, sitting comfortably within the indentations forced into the floor by the weight of its large wooden frame. Breathing a sigh of relief, Liana sat upright and found herself face to face with the young man from Dr. Rattner's reception area. She instantly screamed!

"Who are you?" she shouted. "What are you doing here?"

Liana pulled the sheets up to her neck, as if they could protect her from imminent danger. He was odd. Everything about him was odd; dark eyes hid underneath the shadows of his prominent brow, human hair still threaded across his leathery clothes—*although this time it was red, not blonde*—and his smile beamed off a gloomy face as though it had been stolen from Ronald McDonald.

"I said, 'What are you doing here?'" shouted Liana.

"Me?" he said.

"Yes, you!"

Strange, his exterior was so dark and threatening, but his personality was quite the opposite.

"You can see me?" he said.

"Get out!"

No sooner did the words leave her mouth than she leapt out of her bed, darted over to her vanity, grabbed a very threatening-looking pink hair dryer, and pointed it at him as if brandishing a semiautomatic firearm.

The man jumped back, "No, wait. Let me explain."

"Get out!"

Her bedroom door swung open, revealing Jamison the Great, wearing a navy blue bathrobe and armed with a 1940s tennis racket. His hair perched high above his left ear like the neck of a swan.

"Liana, is everything okay?"

"No! Make him go away!"

Jamison looked directly at the young man. The creases in his brow grew longer and darker as his eyes zeroed in on the perpetrator.

"Who?" said Jamison.

"Him! Right in front of you."

Jamison, eyes still laser-focused, scanned the room for any

signs of life.

"Liana, I don't see anyone."

The young man smirked at him.

"What?" said Liana. "He's right there. He's smiling at you."

Jumping at an opportunity to antagonize, the young man waved his hands in Jamison's face.

"Now he's waving at you."

Again, his face had changed. What juicy emotion was he drowning in behind those tired eyes? I wanted to feel it, too.

Jamison lowered his racket and closed his eyes. If eyes were, indeed, the windows of the mind, this particular set would reveal that point in a person's head where impulse meets reason. That split second where you must choose between two roads: that of base instinctual impulse, a tool used for survival by fight or flight, or that of reason, a tool used for survival by compromise, the more powerful being the former. Jamison had found himself at this crossroads many times before, almost always in the company of his wife. Luckily for him, the discipline of magic had inadvertently prepared him for these moments. It would sometimes take years of practicing to perfect a single illusion. And in the moments where he simply could've given up, given in to his impulse and thrown the cards on the floor, he'd instead chosen to continue on.

Of course, there were the moments where he failed, like the

night he threw an entire turkey dinner off the second-floor balcony to prove to his wife that the turkey was, in fact, dead and could not fly. But he did choose to stay with her, to see her through until the end. What would he do now? Now that he was faced with another beginning?

"I don't see anyone," said Jamison. "Are you feeling okay?"

"Yes, I..." Liana watched the young man saunter over to her windowsill to perch. "I guess I must have been dreaming."

She lowered her hair dryer in defeat.

"It's okay, dear, just try to get back to sleep."

He walked over to her bedroom door and exited.

Liana stood in silence for a moment, wondering whether the perpetrator was still there.

"That was fun!" said the young man.

Liana climbed back into bed and closed her eyes.

"I wasn't sure how that was going to go, but I think you handled it well, considering."

Liana opened her eyes and looked at the bottle of pills on her nightstand. *Should she take another one?*

"Hello?" said the young man.

He left the windowsill and cautiously stepped closer to get a better look at her eyes. Liana turned her head further out of sight.

"Are you ignoring me?" he said. Liana remained still. "That's fine, I can do the talking."

Still unsure of her consciousness, he crouched down to look directly at her face.

"You can still hear me, right?"

Liana remained still.

"Well, if you cannot see or hear me, I guess it's okay for me to do this." The young man leaned over to kiss Liana on the lips.

"Get away from me!" she said.

Again, Liana leapt out of her bed and backed up against the wall.

"She's alive!" said the young man.

While incredibly annoying and glib, Liana preferred this to the alternative of threatening and scary and was oddly at ease. She began to pace across the left side of her room, as if claiming her territory.

"Listen," she started, "I don't know who or what you are—

"You can call me Taffi,"

Liana stopped and scowled at him.

"Taffi?" she said, "The horse? You're named after a horse?"

"What?" he said. "No."

"Now I know this is all in my head."

Liana resumed pacing, this time on the right side of the room. Taffi rounded the edge of the bed to get closer and triumphantly declared, "Taffi is not my real name."

"No? Then what is it, Cotton Candy?"

"No, I can't tell you."

"Why not?"

"I didn't make the rules; I just can't."

As Liana was now almost certain that none of this was actually happening, she looked over at the bottle of medication on her bedside table. Surely, she could take another one, or maybe even two. It was clear that one by itself was not enough.

"I'm a genie!" shouted Taffi.

Liana looked at him for a moment. She thought back to that day at school when her friend Rachel fell down the stairs. *Or did she push her?* Her teacher was talking about genies just before it happened. First, the name of the horse, then the mention of genies…were these all signs that her illness was getting worse by the minute? The symptoms came rushing into her head, like experiencing some sort of withdrawal from the absence of blissful denial. The room began to spin.

"I said, 'I'm a genie,'" repeated Taffi.

"Then I wish you would go away," said Liana.

"It doesn't work like that."

Liana began breathing more heavily. She fell back into bed and closed her eyes. Beads of sweat started rolling down her forehead as she pulled the closest corner of her soft purple sheet. Taffi saw that she was weak and seized the opportunity to regain the dominant role in their rapidly failing encounter. Just as Liana pulled up the final corner of her sheet, Taffi slid his leg underneath it, like slipping on a boot, entered the bed, and laid his head on her pillow.

"Go away!'" Liana said as she began to cry.

Taffi's mischievous grin faded into a nondescript frown. *I could feel him. I saw Liana through his eyes and became as confused as he was.* Normally, he would relish making a girl cry. After all, his role was to make life as difficult and unnerving as possible for humans. Not to cause death or destruction, not him, but just to "poke the bear" as they say. But this time was different. He felt no satisfaction or sense of accomplishment. He would surely not share this encounter with his father, or if he did, it would be told with an entirely slanted point of view. He almost wished he could take it back. Perhaps if he hadn't jumped into bed, she would still be having fun. Or maybe she wasn't having fun at all. Wait a minute, why did he care if she was having fun? Was it because she could see him, because she noticed him? · This kind of thing had never happened before, a human seeing a genie, unless of course the genie wanted to be seen, which he didn't. *Or did he?*

"You know," he started, "humans aren't supposed to be able to see genies."

Liana, head still buried in her hands, mumbled, "Then why

can I see you?"

Taffi sat up. "Because you're not human."

Liana looked up at him with streaks of tears on her cheeks. Taffi smiled at her and extended his hand.

"I really am crazy," she said softly.

Taffi quickly pulled his hand back.

"No," he said, "I mean not completely human. My father told me about this, but I didn't think it was true. You saw me this morning, didn't you, during coffee?"

"No," said Liana.

"You did! You looked right at me."

Liana chose to ignore him, and with no illusions left to cling to, she slowly slid back under the covers. She laid there hopeless, helpless, almost catatonic.

Taffi regained the dominant role between the two of them and felt all the burdens that came with it. Anxiety and uncertainty weighed down on him like a heavy fog. He couldn't decide; should he cross that line? Should he go against his better judgment, or worse, the judgment of his father, and tell her what he knew? His heartbeat quickened. What would the consequences be? Banishment, servitude, or worst of all, binding? And what would become of her?

Taffi stopped thinking for a moment and looked at her. She was so sad, so defeated. Was this all too much for her? Did she regret seeing him? Was he asking too much or not giving enough? Maybe she wasn't ready, or maybe he wasn't ready. And then he thought about what her life would be like if he had never approached her. She would be safe, content enough, and her father would be able to live the rest of his life in peace. No ripples in the water, no flickering of the flame, just peace.

"It is a legend among my kind that a human with genie blood descended from a mixed union—from a genie and a human mating," said Taffi. "Of course, no one ever believed it, but you, you can see me!"

He didn't know why he said it. It was, undoubtedly, completely selfish. Whether his decision to tell her was out of his need to be mischievous or his need to be noticed, neither was met by Liana's response.

"Go away," she said in a soft monotone voice.

Taffi was stunned into silence.

"No, didn't you hear what I just said? You have genie blood in you!"

Liana's face tightened in emotional agony as she closed her eyes.

"Leave me alone!"

Taffi whipped open the covers of her bed like a matador taunting a bull.

"You don't understand. If others find out, they'll come for you."

As Taffi reached out to touch her, Liana promptly vaulted into an upright position and pushed him off her bed.

"Stop it! Get out of my head!"

Liana threw her pillow at him, then the bottle of pills, and then the glass of water from her bedside table. Taffi dodged each item successfully, forcing the glass to crash into pieces on the bedroom floor.

"Get out!" she shouted again and again, this time accompanied by handfuls of loose change from the glass jar on the same bedside table.

Tired of dancing around the tiny groups of weaponized currency, Taffi reached out his hand to bat away the next batch. He caught a few pennies to return the assault. Liana stopped and looked at his hand. She could see the pennies through a gap between his thumb and forefinger resting against the crescent shape of his palm. Oddly, they almost immediately began to sizzle. Taffi threw the change to the floor and hid his hand behind his back. Then, Liana realized it wasn't the pennies that sizzled; it was his hand. Taffi started to back away toward the window.

"What happened?" said Liana.

She immediately felt herself falling back under the spell of that blissful denial, and, as that question came out of her mouth, she wished she could've pulled it right back in.

"Nothing happened," he said. "I'm fine. I have to go."

Liana said nothing; she only watched as he climbed into the frame of the open window. And then, a final reminder of her psychosis, she saw a tattoo of ancient script on the back of his neck, just like the one on the faceless man in her dream and on her father's stagehand, Stefan. Was this her illness, or was there something real happening here? As Taffi was almost gone, she didn't have time to make a decision.

"Wait!" she said, but it was too late; he was gone.

Her mood of despair had suddenly turned to one of intrigue. Either her schizophrenia was in and of itself a master of creating thrills and suspense, or she had discovered a tangible way to combat these strange experiences, or both. Liana walked over to the loose change lying on the floor where it had singed the hallucination otherwise known as Taffi. She knelt on the floor and began picking up the scattered debris from her battle: the pillow, the broken shards of glass, the loose change, and finally, the pills from her bottle of meds, each of which had rolled to its own strategic hiding spot— under the rug, under the bed, behind the dresser, mixed in with the puddle of water from the broken glass, in between the crack of the decades-old, hard wooden floor, and stuck in the air vent. And while, in accepting her diagnosis, she touched the cold, unforgiving surface of "rock bottom," doubt was lurking somewhere in the back of her mind—maybe she wasn't sick; maybe it was all real.

Chapter 9

A TURTLENECK

In a match often too close to call, Liana had wrestled with reality in a timeless vacuum inside her head. It was a nail biter: cold sweats, insomnia, scattered voices, and fragmented dreams, all culminating to this point, to this climax, and all put to a halt by a turtleneck.

Stefan, in a black turtleneck, walked across the stage at the pace of his garment's inspiration, like he had specifically chosen this outer shell as a reflection of his inner self. Liana, as it were, could not see the back of his neck. The purpose of her visit had been thwarted. Now what? Jamison was not there. She looked around for some other excuse, an alibi. Surely someone would ask her what she was doing there, and the truth would only come back to her father and then her therapist.

Several anonymous stagehands and building workers buzzed like busy bees around the countless pulleys and wrinkled backdrops. One of the backdrops caught Liana's eye, a large ship with the name *The Drunken Maiden* written across the side. She walked toward it until one of the busy bees, an older security guard, stumbled into her like a depraved zombie.

"Ow!" said Liana.

"Oh, I'm so sorry," said the security guard.

Oh, no, thought Liana. She hadn't come up with anything yet. What was she going to tell him? Her heart began to pound, as if keeping the thunderous beat of some obnoxious death metal song. Bracing for an interrogation, Liana held her breath.

"I just got off the night shift and can barely keep my eyes open," said the security guard. "They say a day spot might open up in a couple of weeks. I hope I can make it till then."

He tried to mask a long laborious yawn with his shaky old man hands and then off he went.

Liana exhaled in relief. It didn't occur to her that perhaps no one cared she was there at all.

"Liana?" said Stefan. Liana jumped with a squeal.

"I didn't mean to startle you," he said.

Although Liana's heartbeat immediately ramped back up to death-metal levels, she didn't feel the distaste she had felt when she first met him.

"It's okay!" she blurted. "I'm fine."

Stefan looked at her for a moment, a long moment. *Why was it so long? Was he suspicious, or was this just the normal pace for a conversation with a turtle?* In either case, the silence was too much for Liana to bear.

"It's nice to see you again," she said.

"Yes, likewise," he replied.

Seemingly becoming aware of his awkwardness, Stefan made a feeble attempt to perk up.

"Is everything okay? How's your father? He's still doing the show today, isn't he?"

"Oh, yes, of course," said Liana.

"Good. You had me worried for a second."

He slowly turned away, changing the stance of his feet as if preparing his body for motion. *That was it?* Liana felt her emotional capital building back up and could think of only one thing to spend it on: getting what she came for. She looked at the collar of Stefan's turtleneck as he walked away. It was time to go on the offensive. Liana turned and followed him offstage.

Stefan entered the next room with the satisfaction of a hoarder returning to his nest. In fact, according to Jamison, the only reports of ever seeing him smile were at times when he was nestled comfortably among the scattered lumber, various tools, and bolts of muslin in this, his special room. Just as he was about to make another impression of his backside in a pile of sawdust on his chair, Liana bolted in like a superhero.

"Wait, Stefan!" she called.

He turned his head like an owl, and just as quick.

"I wanted to make sure everything was okay with the harness."

"Oh, yes," said Stefan. "I'm so sorry about what happened on opening night. It was a total fluke. I promise it won't happen again. These brand-new harnesses are top-of-the-line."

"Great."

Liana began to notice the subtle tells in his body language and revealing tones of his voice. He was apologetic and submissive and would certainly help her.

"Also," she started, "I know this may seem a little strange, but, that tattoo on the back of your neck; I think I've seen it somewhere else before. What does it mean?"

Stefan smiled. "That old thing? I got it back when I was in high school. I was a wild one back then."

Liana smiled, insisting on another answer.

"It means about ten different things," Stefan obliged.

"Really?"

"Yes, strange, isn't it? Some ancient language, I forget the name of it. I've got a whole book of different translations in the back. Would you like to see it?"

"Sure. I'd love to."

Stefan sauntered over to a large metal cabinet with Liana in tow. He seemed to glide across, around and through the mass of stuff about the room, while Liana dodged everything like navigating an obstacle course.

"My wife says I collect too much crap, so I've started keeping things here at the theater."

He opened the large metal cabinet and began rummaging through piles of old dusty books. The search seemed to go on forever.

"I don't want to be a bother," Liana said trying to come up with a suitable excuse to leave.

"No, don't be silly. It's my pleasure."

Maybe so, but Liana began to regret her actions. The wrestling match wasn't over, and reality had started gaining ground. Without a struggle, Liana gave up her dominant position and started to back away from Stefan. Assuming her place as the submissive, she was afraid to turn away from him and didn't notice the door behind her closing.

"You have her eyes, you know," said Stefan.

"What?"

"Her eyes, the woman in your dreams."

As Liana began to panic, Stefan continued rummaging through the old books.

"How do you know about—?"

"I know everything about you."

He turned to look at her. He was different, no longer the slow-moving turtle but rather a dominant silverback gorilla. His shoulders bulged as his eyes pierced into Liana's mind.

"What do you mean?" said Liana.

"You can see things with those eyes, can't you?" he asked.

Liana backed away as he gained ground on her.

"Amazing things," said Stefan.

His eyes became black, and Liana felt herself going into a trance. Images of the beautiful woman from her dreams and the elder man flashed into her head, she standing on the cliff and he advancing on her. Still, Liana couldn't see his face. Why couldn't she see his face? The images continued to flash, faster and faster; the beautiful woman, the elder man, the hanging man, the laughing band of ruffians, the beautiful woman, the elder man, the beautiful woman, the elder man, the elder man, the elder man. The images stopped. Liana looked directly in front of her and saw his face. It was him.

"Xethalis," she whispered.

Stefan smiled. Liana thrust out her arms and pushed Stefan across the room with the strength of twenty men. His back slammed against the opposite wall, causing it to collapse on top of him.

Liana's trance broke. She looked down at her hands then

across the room at Stefan, buried beneath the collapsed wall.

Chapter 10

SIX STICHES

Once again, serious men of stature hanging on the wall peered down at Liana in judgment. Everywhere she moved, they followed, all taking their cues from Dr. Rattner. She sat across from Liana, wearing that same green suit that matched the room so perfectly. *Why was she wearing the same suit? Surely she has other suits, or even a nice dress or two. Maybe it was a different suit, just a shade darker or lighter than the last.* Liana's mind continued to wander as she sat in judgment. This was supposed to be a safe place, a place of acceptance, so why did she feel judged? Was this Dr. Rattner's intent? To make Liana feel as though she'd committed a crime? As though allowing herself to be taken over by her psychosis was like falling off the wagon after being sober for a month. Was she slipping down that famed slope to a life of deviance? She was no addict. *Or was she?* Was there any difference between the calm euphoria one gets from a mind-altering substance and the calm sense of purpose Liana got from her visions and dreams? Both are security blankets, meant to warm one from the chill of harsh, relentless reality. Yes, then, Liana had committed a crime. What would her sentence be? More drugs? A visit to an institution? The loss of her father? But wait, she did push Stefan across the room. That was no vision or dream, although she did not remember it. There was actual physical evidence. The wall did crumble, and Stefan was in the hospital with stitches on the back of his head, six to be exact.

"Sometimes," started Dr. Rattner, "when we're faced with seemingly life or death situations, our adrenaline kicks in, and we can have great strength."

"Okay," replied Liana.

She had heard of people lifting cars and such to save children, so that was believable.

"What about the tattoo?" she said.

Dr. Rattner leaned forward, "Liana, your mind is playing tricks on you. It may take several days for the medicine to take effect. But I promise—"

"Don't listen to her," whispered Taffi. He was suddenly standing behind Dr. Rattner's large, ominous chair.

"Once it does, you won't have any more of these visions," finished Dr. Rattner.

Liana gazed at Taffi like a deer in headlights.

"Liana?" called Dr. Rattner.

"Yes."

"Are you seeing someone else in the room right now?"

"Yes."

"Liana," started Taffi, as he rounded to the front of the chair, "You have to listen to me; she's not who she says she is. She's a genie."

"What's he saying?" said Dr. Rattner.

"He says you're a genie," Liana said.

"Why do you want me to be a genie?"

"It's not me; it's him."

She pointed to Taffi, who began to look around the room as if searching for something. Liana, somehow, was completely calm. Taffi, on the other hand, was screaming panic through his body language.

"Just get up and leave!" he said.

Dr. Rattner leaned back against her chair and reached inside the pocket of her suit coat.

"You know," said Dr. Rattner, "I have a son just like Taffi."

As she spoke, Dr. Rattner slowly pulled a silver cigarette holder and accompanying lighter from her pocket. "Always getting into trouble, never listening to me." She placed a cigarette in her mouth and raised the burning end of the lighter up toward her lips. "He's the perfect rebel."

She lit the cigarette and slowly pulled the smoke into her

mouth and down into the furthest depths of her lungs. Taffi stared at her, as if waiting for some kind of attack. Dr. Rattner exhaled the smoke for what seemed like several minutes, filling the room with a dense fog.

"Is that why you created him?" said Dr. Rattner. "To rebel against your parents? Your mother was in and out of mental institutions throughout your childhood. You said Taffi was picking on your father. Is that what you want? To get back at him for making your mother sick?"

Liana thought for a moment. The fog in the room started to clear. *Could that be it?* Was she subconsciously lashing out to somehow reconcile the painful memories of her childhood? She looked back at Dr. Rattner, and the cigarette was gone. None of it was real. There was no smell of cigarette smoke, no lighter, and even the serious framed men on the walls seemed to be looking the other way. She didn't think that her childhood was that bad, but perhaps it was too much for her.

"I'm sorry," said Liana.

"No need to apologize, dear."

She turned her head for a moment, and Liana noticed some stitches poking out of the hair on the back of her head—six of them to be exact. As Liana examined the stitches from afar, a sensation of clarity flooded into her head.

"How did you know his name?" said Liana.

"Whose name?" said Dr. Rattner.

Liana slowly stood up from her chair.

"I never told you his name. Taffi. How did you know?"

Dr. Rattner smiled. She was once again at a crossroads; should she continue on this road of therapy and medication, or should she take more aggressive action?

"I know because I named him," she answered. "A name fit for a boy just as stupid and stubborn as a horse."

Dr. Rattner had made her decision. She was tired of this hopeless charade. It worked with Liana's mother, but Liana was different, stronger—*like I knew she would be*. More smoke blew out of her mouth, orbiting around her face like a tornado. Liana backed away toward Taffi, who was still bracing for some kind of impact. The smoke swept the folds of skin around Dr. Rattner's face like an overstretched membrane that was released from its vessel, only to be pulled and contorted to fit another. Her eyebrows grew out like a thousand little centipede legs moving in harmony to the rhythm of the smoke. The tornado grew bigger and bigger until it swept up all the serious framed men from the walls.

"What's happening!" said Liana.

Everything suddenly froze. The pictures from the wall, suspended in midair, all turned to stare at Liana, once again in judgment. Behind them was no longer a well-put-together, educated woman in matching attire but rather the dark-eyed, sullen Stefan, dressed in a dark cloak. This was not the turtle Stefan; it was the silverback gorilla Stefan. Taffi jumped in front of Liana.

"She's mine!" he said.

"You forget your place, boy," replied Stefan.

Liana ran to the office door, but it was locked. She looked back at the two men, each gazing at her like a trophy to be won—or worse, taken. Stefan's gaze was pure darkness, while Taffi's was like that of a jilted sibling who was about to lose his toy; neither one was appealing.

"Get away from me!" she said. "I don't belong to anyone."

"Oh, but you do, my dear," said Stefan. "You're a human."

Liana collapsed in the corner by the door. Although she tried, she could no longer find reason; she could no longer calculate her next action. It was fight or flight, and while she chose the latter, there was still nowhere to run.

"She's not human!" said Taffi.

Stefan looked at him with disdain.

"You think because she can see us she's special?" said Stefan. "She's just like her mother."

"What?" said Liana.

All at once, Liana's curiosity took over, so much so that it was somehow able to override her fear. She stood up straight and gazed back at Stefan with defiance. As valiant as she was trying to be, Stefan still did not back down; he didn't even flinch.

"You inherited a broken mind, Liana," mocked Stefan. "None of this is real."

Liana once again found herself going into a trance.

"Don't listen to him," said Taffi.

"Good night, Liana," whispered Stefan, as his eyes began to glow.

"I won't let you touch her!" said Taffi.

As he ran toward him, Stefan reached under his cloak, grabbed what looked like a baseball-sized penny, and threw it at Taffi's chest, knocking him to the floor.

"Goodbye, son," muttered Stefan.

Taffi lay on the floor writhing in pain, as if pinned down by the weight of a steamroller. A blinding flash of light lit up the office and then vanished along with Liana, Taffi, and Stefan.

Chapter **11**

THE BIG TALK

A large ball of dark orange flames peered across the top of the ocean, one last glance before disappearing into the night. And while it could see everything—seagulls, half-eaten coconuts, tiny grains of sand, and the tips of seaweed reaching up to touch the sky from the dark ocean floor—the sun's glow seemed to focus in on two figures embracing on the beach.

"Did you tell him?" said Alexander.

I laid my back against his chest. Unable to look each other in the eyes, we stared attentively at the setting sun. I didn't know how to respond. Of course, I knew the answer, but so did he. It was a "big talk." The kind of talk that, once completed, the reaction would be such that everyone would know the outcome without having to ask. Like a teenage girl telling her parents she's pregnant, or a teenage boy coming out to his parents, the result is always the same—either big hugs or angry rants.

"Yes," I said.

Now another "big talk" had begun. Alexander tried to look at me, but I was lost in my head. Traditionally, the man is supposed to take all the risks and provide comfort and stability. So far, all he'd brought was

inaction and uncertainty, although it wasn't for lack of effort or desire;
this was a strange land, and he was powerless in it.

"He was very upset," I said. "I knew I couldn't trust him."

"I'm sorry," said Alexander.

He turned toward the sun as if looking for something or someone.
Perhaps he wondered whether he was being watched.

"He is your father," said Alexander.

I corrected him, "I'm only a piece of property to him. He's wanted
me to marry that man since I was born. Peace between our two families is
more important to him than my happiness."

Alexander's shoulders sank into a concave chest.

"Does this mean they'll keep fighting?" he asked.

"Yes."

"Will your family be hurt?"

"Yes."

Alexander peered back up at the sun. What was he thinking? There
were only two possible answers: give me the love that my family never
could, or save the lives of my family. Both were noble and just but also had
devastating consequences. How do you choose between love lost and lives
lost?

He got up as the last sliver of sunlight disappeared into the ocean,
"I'm sorry. Maybe this was a bad idea. Maybe I should've never come
here."

He turned his head from the sun and began to walk away.

"Wait!" I said as I leapt up and started after him. "Please, wait. I knew the risks, what my family might think. I did this for you. Don't you understand that?"

Alexander stopped and turned toward me. He had made his choice. This was it. This was the part where he was supposed to make me see that he wasn't worth it, that he wasn't who I thought he was, the sacrificial charade meant to save something greater than himself.

"Your family will never accept me," he admitted, "the pain I've caused them. I'm not one of them."

"I don't care. We'll make our own family."

I reached out for his hand, but he held it back. Tears welled up in his eyes.

"No! I'm not coming between you and your family."

I watched him as he walked away into the distance. It wasn't until then, the moment he turned away from me, that any doubt I had was erased from my mind. The men in my world went to war over property. Not one of them ever had the strength to risk losing for something bigger than himself. Perhaps Alexander was stronger than them after all.

"I'm pregnant!" I said.

Alexander stopped and smiled back at me.

"What?" he said.

I smiled back at him.

"I'm pregnant."

Tears flew off his face as he ran toward me, faster than his shadow could keep up. We met in the spotlight of the moon shining overhead. I took his hand and placed it on my belly.

"We're going to have a baby."

Chapter **12**

RACKET AND ROBE

Liana's head jerked away from her pillow like she was doing the final sit-up of some mind-numbing abs workout. The dreams were much more frequent now. They were more like visions than dreams. Dreams were supposed to be enigmatic and metaphorical; these were like sequential events where the people meant what they said and said what they meant, each night a new chapter unfolding like an episodic television show. The only thing cryptic about them was how, after several days on her medication, the visions or dreams or whatever they were, were getting worse.

The last thing Liana remembered was the blinding flash of light in Dr. Rattner's office. Or was it Stefan's office? Maybe it was all part of her dream. She glanced to her left and found Taffi lying next to her in bed.

Liana screamed!

Taffi awoke and leapt off her bed.

"What?!" he said, "What's happening?"

Liana examined his face. It was sullen and pale, like Stefan's.

"How did you get in here?" she said.

"What?"

Taffi looked around the room for something familiar, something to help him identify his location.

"I don't know," he continued. "We were in the office—"

"I don't belong to you!" said Liana.

"What?!"

The suggestion of human property must've jogged Taffi's memory, as his face turned from one of disgust to surprising guilt. He looked down at his chest to find a large copper emblem burned into his skin.

"I didn't do this," he said.

A voice rang out from the distance, "Liana?"

It was Jamison. He, at this point, was no stranger to routine shouting through all hours of the night, first with his wife, and now with Liana.

"Who's in there?" he asked.

Although not yet present in the room, the mere anticipation of his entrance gave Liana permission to go on the offense.

"Get him away from me!" she said.

"I'm not even near you," said Taffi.

Jamison entered triumphant, sure that his well-rehearsed monologue about reality and fantasy would quell yet another night of schizophrenic ramblings. After almost a decade, with Liana present at every awkward, inappropriate, and sometimes terrifying moment, he had perfected this calm, reassuring performance to keep the peace in his family. Even his choice of attire was in on it: the blue bathrobe and vintage tennis racket. Each had its purpose: the blue bathrobe, once dark navy blue, allowed the distressed to maintain their dignity by suggesting that Jamison was not so worried that he didn't have time to put on a bathrobe to protect his modesty, while the vintage tennis racket suggested that, while he wasn't overly worried, he would still risk even his most sentimental gifts for the safety of his loved ones. Oh, the stories these inanimate objects could tell. What would it be this time? A hallucination? A disembodied voice? The two were so rich with experience they could have their own spinoff: "Racket and Robe: Tales from an Unlikely Pair of Night Watchmen."

"Who are you?!" said Jamison, "What are you doing here!?"

Liana looked at him and felt relief for the first time in years.

"You can see him?" she asked. "I told you; I'm not crazy!"

For Jamison, this was also a first, but his sunken eyes and furrowed brow suggested a different kind of feeling, one of shock and nausea.

"Where's my daughter?" he said.

Now Taffi was having a first experience, and like Jamison's, it seemed to be one of complete shock.

"Are you talking to me?" he asked.

"Don't play games with me, son," Jamison said.

As if being struck by some kind of blunt force, Taffi convulsed and reached for the emblem on his chest.

"Dad, I'm right here," said Liana. She tried to grab her father's hand, but it passed right through.

"Can't you see her?" said Taffi.

As this was unscripted territory, Jamison's improvisational skills proved to be less than excellent. I was certain his mind was too old to grapple with all the possibilities that presented themselves. Were Liana and his wife right all along? Was this young man a genie like his daughter had said? Was this all just a coincidence? Was this event completely random and totally unrelated to his family's history?

"Enough!" said Jamison, "What did you do with my daughter?"

"Nothing!" replied Taffi.

Liana positioned herself in between the two men.

"Dad," she started. "I'm standing right in front of you."

But he could not see her. Despite his age, Jamison's adrenaline was alive and well within him. He lunged and swung his racket at Taffi. After years of false alarms, racket and robe had finally gotten some action.

"Dad, stop!" said Liana, but it was useless.

She looked into his eyes as they became glossy with tears. She could not imagine what he was feeling.

"Tell me where she is!" said Jamison.

He swung again and again, each time passing through Liana's body like a plane through a cloud. Taffi mustered what little strength he had to dodge each passing attack, finally seeking refuge through the open window.

"Come back here!" said Jamison.

Too frail to leap out of the second-story window, Jamison ran out of Liana's bedroom and down the stairs toward the front door of the house.

"Dad, wait!" said Liana.

Taffi lay on the ground just outside Liana's window. Jamison promptly exited the house and continued the charge on Taffi.

"Tell me where she is!" Jamison said, as he prepared his racket for another blow.

"Dad, stop!" Liana screamed, hoping the louder she spoke, the better chance he had of hearing her.

Jamison swung again, missing his target and decapitating a nearby hydrangea.

Both men were now clutching their chests, each for a very different reason. Taffi saw his opportunity to escape and ran off toward a nearby park. Liana didn't know what to do.

"Dad? Can you hear me?" she whispered.

He, of course, could not. After a few moments, Jamison hurried back inside the house to contact the authorities, and Liana remained on their front lawn. She couldn't just leave him; someone had to look after him, especially now. She remembered his shaking hand, the stiff back, and the harness. Someone had to make sure there were no accidents. And as she thought, Liana realized that perhaps she was the accident. *Was it all her fault? Was she turning into her...?* Liana couldn't bear the thought. No, she wasn't leaving him; she was just going to get help.

Liana stood up and looked at her father pacing back and forth through the kitchen window. She felt powerless, like Alexander. *Was this a test? Was she being watched?* Liana looked toward the park and took her first step.

Chapter 13

SUNDAY IN THE PARK

The house got smaller and smaller with each step Liana took. Soon it faded into obscurity along with the other houses on the block, it was just another dot of color on the canvas. It sat comfortably among the old Tudor, Victorian, and Colonial houses in their upper-class suburban neighborhood. It was a commuter town, only 30 minutes from New York City by car, 40 by train. It wasn't gaudy like the McMansions of the '80s and '90s but rather a smaller, more compact version of the grand estates from the early 1900s. The elegance of each house varied from one to the next; still there remained an unspoken level of appropriate style and upkeep that was never breached.

It was a requirement for any town such as this to have a park nearby, not by law, but by demand. The park was perfectly landscaped and engineered to provide both an escape from civilization and a playground for the weekend warriors. Liana peered into it, trying to distinguish one object from the next, hoping to come across Taffi. Lit only by a single street lamp, the park appeared vaguely spotted, like a living Georges Seurat painting. Each bush or tree was distinctly its own but somehow still faded into the others, as though they were all connected.

As Liana moved closer, she began to distinguish dark shadows from dark objects. Finally, she spotted what looked like a wounded animal, curled up in the fetal position, lying against a large tree. Without entertaining the notion that it might actually be a wounded animal, Liana ran toward it.

"What did you do to me?" she screamed. Lucky for her, it was indeed Taffi, still clutching the copper emblem on his chest.

"Nothing," he replied.

"Don't lie to me! My father is old. He can't handle this. Make it stop!"

"I can't," he said.

"I'll do whatever you want me to," said Liana. "Just make it stop!"

Taffi's pain, while still significant, suddenly took a back seat to this new proposition. Her offer, total submission, was at the very center of the genie-human conflict. Genies had untold godlike powers for centuries, with egos to match. The difference in capability and awareness between the two was like that of a human and a dog. Dogs, while compassionate and intelligent, cannot reason and, as such, could never comprehend the ability to do so. In much the same way, humans cannot manipulate time and space and therefore have no comprehension of it. Like dogs, humans are naturally submissive to genies but for one small caveat: binding. The binding of a genie reverses the natural order, making the human dominant. Taffi could have accepted her offer, but he did not.

"I said make it stop!" cried Liana.

"I told you, I can't!"

Liana sat next to him, knee to knee. Her pants brushed against the living threads of his vinyl garment.

"Please," she said softly.

Taffi looked at her curiously, then adoringly, but only for a moment. Had Liana's tactic worked? Taffi was warned about such games that humans play. All genies were taught from a young age not to be fooled by the allure of human compassion. Yet there was always a little voice whispering in the back of their minds: What if it was real, and not just a trick? Like a powerful drug, this small hint of a possibility cast a shadow over Taffi's better judgment. He felt the need to be honest with her.

"You've been cursed," said Taffi.

"What?"

"My father, he has made you invisible to human eyes. It is a curse."

"No," Liana said softly. This wasn't what she was hoping to

hear.

"This has happened before, the man you call Jimmy Hoffa, the woman who killed Kennedy, the little boy who lived at the end of your block—they were all cursed like you."

As he spoke, Liana's heart began to race and her breath quickened. I could feel the pulsing through her veins that wrapped around her ankle. She stood up and began pacing as she did the night they first met in her bedroom.

"No, they're all just missing. This isn't happening to me. I just need my medicine." She began to walk away.

"That won't help you!" shouted Taffi.

Liana began to run toward her house.

"Get out of my head!"

Taffi climbed to his feet. "Liana!" Stop! Please let me explain!"

A disembodied voice echoed him from a distance.

"Liana, wait!"

Liana stopped and looked back at Taffi. The voice's owner, a privileged neighborhood teen out looking for trouble, joined Taffi at his side.

"Who you talking to?" said another neighborhood teen.

They had multiplied. Three neighborhood teens in all had surrounded Taffi.

"No one," replied Taffi.

The teens laughed. They had on the signature jock uniform: a T-shirt with the latest local sports champions bottomed off by a pair of $400 jeans that came pre-worn. Spotty beards poked out of their soft faces, the thickness of which was in direct correlation to the group's pecking order: the leader with the fullest beard and the grunt with the sparsest. Their combined fragrance, one of "just for men" bar soap and cheap whiskey, stunned Taffi's senses as they got closer. Liana watched the scene unfold from afar, a budget Iron Man surrounded by a junior varsity tennis team.

"Oh, come on," started the head teen, "you were talking to someone."

Taffi tried to sneak by them but was blocked each time by the tightening of their circle.

"Liana," said the grunt teen.

"Yeah, Liana," echoed the head teen. "Where is she?"

"I was just talking to myself," replied Taffi.

The middle teen, completely docile up to this point, suddenly shoved Taffi onto the ground.

"Is she pretty?" asked the middle teen.

"Leave him alone!" said Liana.

Taffi looked over toward her. She was as surprised as he was. What was she doing? The grunt teen kicked Taffi in the stomach.

"Hey!" said Liana, "Leave him alone!"

"They can't hear you," said Taffi.

"Oh, man, he is crazy," said the head teen.

As Liana looked on, her feeling of panic evolved into one of anger. It wasn't right. Taffi had done nothing wrong. There are few moments in life where things are not blurred into a subjective gray area, and this was one of them. It was black and white, the decision clear—she had to help him. Liana rushed toward the action. She wasn't sure what she was going to do once she got there, but she could no longer bear witness to the abuse.

"You got any money, crazy man?" asked the head teen.

"What's the matter with you?" Liana asked Taffi. "Fight back!"

He looked up. This second dose of compassion ignited his anger.

"Gladly," said Taffi as he bounced up from the ground and swung wildly at the middle teen, missing him completely.

"Whoa!" said the middle teen, "we've got a wild one here."

He struck Taffi in the face, sending him back to the ground. The other teens laughed.

"Why are you letting them do this to you?" asked Liana. "Turn them into frogs or something."

Taffi looked at her, blood streaming from his left eye.

"I can't."

"You can't what?" asked the grunt teen.

"Turn you into a frog."

The middle teen and grunt teen pinned Taffi down on the ground as the head teen began to rummage through his clothes.

"Stop it!" said Liana. "Leave him alone!"

She reached for the head teen, but her hands passed right through him, just like they did with her father. She tried again and again, each time with the same result. She could see that Taffi was in pain, but she didn't know what to do. Liana looked around for help; maybe there was someone out walking his dog who could call the police. In her frantic search, she noticed a heavy rock on the ground. Without thinking, Liana grabbed it and slammed it into the back of the head teen. It connected!

"Oww! What was that?!" The head teen looked up to find a large rock floating above his head. It began to fall quickly.

"Look out!" said the grunt teen.

The rock dropped from the sky, narrowly missing the head teen but landing squarely between Taffi's legs.

"Aaahh!" Taffi grabbed his groin.

"I'm sorry!" said Liana. "I didn't mean to—"

"You playing funny tricks on us, crazy man?" interrupted the middle teen.

Just as they started back on the offense, Liana picked up the rock again. The teens stared at it as it floated around them.

"Holy crap," said the grunt teen, "are you guys seeing this?"

Before they could answer, Liana raced toward them. The disembodied rock pushed them out of the park like a rancher driving cattle.

Chapter 14

IN IT TOGETHER

A large rock fell to the ground like a shell casing discharged from a rifle after the final shot of battle. Liana watched the three teens retreat back toward their homes, back to safety. She couldn't help but feel a little joy. As much as she hated to admit it, there was something oddly satisfying about making those boys suffer. Was this how bullies felt after picking on someone? Was this how Taffi felt when he was picking on her father? What was it about prodding others that gave some so much satisfaction? Was it vengeance? Vengeance for what?

Liana looked back at Taffi, lying on the ground. Maybe they weren't so different. She couldn't leave him now, now that they shared this moment together. Liana walked toward him, helped him on his feet, and sat with him against the same tree she'd found him clinging to earlier. Not a word was said. They were not yet friends, but no longer enemies. Liana looked at the cut above his left eye and reached out for it. Taffi pulled back.

"Are you okay?" she asked.

"Yes, thank you," he answered. They sat, again, in silence. In the heat of the moment, they had both gone against their conventional wisdom; Taffi had allowed himself to accept her compassion, to desire it, and Liana had allowed herself to help him, even though he had brought her only misery before.

"Why didn't you do something to them?" said Liana.

Taffi pointed to the large copper emblem on his chest.

"What is that?" said Liana.

"A punishment," said Taffi.

"A punishment, for what?"

"For trying to protect you."

"Oh."

While she felt sorry that he was being punished, Liana now felt better about her decision to come to his aid. She supposed they were even. Taffi winced.

"Does it hurt?"

"Yes, we are vulnerable to copper. In my family, when someone misbehaves, they get branded like this."

Liana reached out to touch the copper emblem on his chest.

"We lose our powers," continued Taffi, "it makes us—"

"Human?" interrupted Liana.

"Almost, yes."

Everything was connected; all of the crazy things Liana had

been seeing and hearing were suddenly starting to make sense.

"This is really happening," she said.

"Yes, it is," said Taffi.

Liana sat for a moment. Her questions were finally answered; everything she was experiencing was real. She wasn't crazy or sick or handicapped. She finally had clarity, a clear direction. And although the direction was completely terrifying, Liana felt relieved, but deep within this relief there was sadness and regret, a deep sadness for her mother. Liana imagined what her parents would've been like if they had known the truth, the truth that could have spared them so much conflict and endless nights of self-medicating.

We always think that if things were different, our lives would be perfect, or at least happier. Would they? Or would knowing the hallucinations were, in fact, real have made things worse than they already were? Maybe her mother would have left to find other genies, in which case...other genies, thought Liana.

"Call someone," she said.

Taffi looked at her confused. "What?"

"You must know someone, another genie that can help us."

"There is no one."

"There must be someone. Don't you have any friends?"

"No. My father is Stefan."

"What does that mean?"

"He is like the sheriff in my family. All the genies fear him; they even fear me. They will not help us."

Liana was immediately suspicious. He was, after all, Stefan's son, and if that was any indication of Taffi's moral character, then he was almost certainly lying. She had seen the darkness of Stefan's heart, first in her dreams and then in person. She had seen it with Taffi, too, *or had she?* Taffi did cause mischief, but he had also reached out to her and even tried to protect her. Maybe he was telling the truth. The men in Liana's dream did fear Stefan, all but one—Alexander. Liana looked at Taffi. She couldn't help but feel some sort of parallel was taking place. Alexander was weak and powerless, just as Taffi was now. They were both sitting by a tree with a woman at their side: the beautiful woman, a strong defiant leader, and Liana. The comparison was perfect but for that detail— Liana was not a strong woman. Defiant? Maybe. But strong? Not yet. Not then. She wondered how the story in her dreams would end. Would the beautiful woman's strength be enough to prevail? And if not, if even she couldn't succeed, what would that mean for Liana? Her eyes began to glisten and then fill up with tears. She retreated to the opposite end of the tree.

Taffi moved to sit next to her. He tried to pull Liana's hands away from her eyes, but she shook him off. Again and again, Taffi tried looking into her eyes but was rejected each time.

"Why do you hide it?" said Taffi.

"What?"

"Your eye."

Liana wiped the tears off her cheeks. "My eye?"

"Your left eye, it's different from your right."

After a moment, Liana reached for her left eye and gently took out the blue contact lens to reveal the eye's true color: bright green. Taffi smiled.

"It's beautiful," he said.

"Thank you."

"Only the Marid have eyes like yours," said Taffi.

"What is the Marid?"

"They are another tribe of genie, the most powerful. They live near the water."

Liana immediately remembered that intrusive cliff in her dreams; it was by the water. And the beautiful woman had two different-colored eyes, too, one blue and one green, just like Liana.

"Can they help us?" said Liana.

Taffi suddenly seemed terrified. "No, they would not."

"Why not?"

"Would fire help ice?!"

Liana backed off, turning her face downward as a scolded child would. Taffi's face softened as he looked at her. He had forgotten that she did not know the ways of his world, not yet.

Trying to extend an olive branch, he blurted out, "They do not like my kind." Liana looked back up at him; now he was the one backing down from embarrassment.

"What about me?" she said.

Taffi peeked up at her and into her eyes, those eyes that were so alluring, so mysterious, so coveted, one more hypnotic than the next. He was powerless against the Marid, but she may not be. "Yes, they would help you."

Without missing a beat, Liana stood up. "Then take me to them."

Again, Taffi was terrified. "They will not help you if I am with you."

Proving once again that she was defiant, Liana fired back, "I don't care. Take me to them."

Taffi stood up to meet her. "I don't have my powers. It would be very dangerous."

"We don't have a choice," said Liana, "do we?"

Taffi turned to look back toward Liana's house. If only she had come with him that first night, none of this would have happened. He looked down at his right hand and opened it to reveal the image of two pennies branded into his palm. "We could get hurt."

Liana walked up to Taffi, grabbed him by the shoulders, and

turned him to face her. "I'm already hurting. Please."

She took Taffi's right hand in hers. The penny images of his seared skin pressed up against Liana's palm. It felt cool. There it was again, that human compassion. *Would he let himself go this time? Did he even have a choice?* Each occurrence, each drink of compassion that he took in made him more and more drunk. The more he had, the more he wanted.

"I will take you to them," he agreed.

"Thank you!"

Taffi smiled and grabbed her hand.

"Come on," he said as he pulled her toward the edge of the park.

"Where are we going?"

"To *The Drunken Maiden*," said Taffi. He started to pick up his pace, and Liana followed suit.

"Is she one of the Marid?"

Taffi stopped and looked back at her. "No. She is a cargo boat. They live by the water, remember? She will take us to them."

Chapter 15

PROPS, BACKDROPS, AND A BOTTLE OF CHAMPAGNE

Taffi stood in front of the old theater where Liana's father performed. He looked up at the ornate architecture, seemingly in admiration, but in actuality, he was looking for a way in. He was no longer hunched over in pain nor fatigued but rather erect and enthusiastic. He had a new purpose, a mission driven by the compassion from another. Perhaps Mr. Lennon was right; all you need is love. In this case, it wasn't accompanied by chivalry. Liana approached the theater alone after trailing behind for several blocks. Surely he could have waited for her, thought Liana.

Taffi looked over at her for a moment; she had returned the blue contact lens to her right eye. Liana, still unsure of their destination, looked back at him with irreverence.

"What are we doing here?" she asked.

"Shhhh!" said Taffi. "I need you to go in and open the door for me."

Liana gazed at the heavy wooden door in front of them. Above it a sign read: Stage Door.

"I don't have a key," she said.

"Just walk through the door," snapped Taffi.

Liana's eyes fell from the door to Taffi with disdain. She had begun to regret her kindness toward him. After following him blindly on a wild goose chase, only to be left behind and finally snapped at once reaching the destination, Taffi had proved to be a jerk.

"Are you kidding?" she said.

Completely missing Liana's facial cues, Taffi replied, "Your curse allows you to pass though objects."

Liana became too intrigued to stay mad.

"Like I did to my father and the guy in the park?"

"Not quite. While you can choose to pass through or touch objects and other genies, you can only pass through humans.

Liana thought for a moment. While this did brighten her mood, she didn't want to let him off the hook that easily.

"Okay," she said in her snottiest tone, "but aren't we supposed to be looking for a boat?"

"We are. Trust me."

Too tired to argue, Liana reached out for the stage door and touched it. Nothing happened. Liana looked back at Taffi primed with another snotty comeback, but before she could launch her verbal attack, she leaned on the door and fell right through.

Liana stood up and found herself backstage. She looked around at the various backdrops, ropes, and pulleys, all lit by the dull red glow of the emergency exit sign. Liana's eyes brought her to the door of Stefan's room, now blocked off by yellow caution tape. She remembered being inside, Stefan coming toward her, and then—

"Hey," shouted Taffi, "open the door!"

Liana came back from her memories and opened the door. Without any gratitude or acknowledgement, Taffi bolted in.

"This way," he said.

Liana's inner child came out, as it often does when one is too tired to reason, and she decided to stay put. *If he had so much energy, then he could find* The Drunken Maiden *by himself.*

Taffi began rifling through the set pieces and backdrops.

"The Marid will help us bind my father to an object," he said. "Once this is done, he must do whatever we wish."

The adult within Liana suddenly perked up. "So that's where the wishes come in."

Taffi heard her but said nothing. *Typical human. Only ever interested in what they can get from others. Would his father be right? Would she, in the end, only want him for the wishes he could grant?* Taffi thought again about how he had let himself be taken by that temptress compassion. And yet, even knowing its deceptive hold, he still could not give up even the possibility that he might get it again.

"Right?" said Liana.

Taffi came back from his thoughts. "Yes. It's a very difficult task. You must know the true name of the genie and possess a piece of his person."

"That should be easy."

Taffi rolled his eyes. *She is so naïve.* "Both are almost impossible to get."

"But you're his son; you must know his true name."

This time Taffi stopped searching and turned around to confront her. "No. We do not share our true names."

Liana again returned to that five-year-old version of herself, but this time she was frightened, not exacerbated. She felt scolded, ashamed that she knew so little about such a major part of her life. Yet what kind of a life was it when you couldn't even trust your own son with your true name? Taffi's gaze remained fixed on her. Perhaps he was thinking the same thing: *why didn't his father trust him?*

"I'm sorry," said Liana.

Taffi broke his gaze and continued to rummage through the backdrops.

"Even when both the true name and personal item are obtained, only the most skilled person can accomplish the binding," said Taffi. His hands passed over a stretched-out piece of muslin tacked to a large wooden frame. "Aha! Give me a hand."

Liana helped Taffi pull out three set pieces, all part of what looked like a shipping dock.

"Put this over there," he said.

Liana took a large piece of wood from him and struggled to attach it to the large wooden frame with the pulled muslin.

Taffi, for the first time, noticed her struggling. She must be very tired, he thought, and he needed her to be in top condition when they finally met the Marid. "Here, let me do it."

Liana handed him the set piece. "Thank you."

"Why don't you take a rest?"

Liana smiled. This was the first time he had acknowledged her physical well-being since the park. "Okay."

She watched him in silence. He wasn't sweating or breathing heavily; that must just be a human thing. Again, she noticed the tattoo on the back of his neck, just like his father's.

"What does it mean?" said Liana.

"What?"

"The tattoo on your neck."

Taffi stopped working for moment. "Oh, that is the mark of the Ifrit."

"What is that?"

"That's the name of my tribe."

"That's why your father had it, too?"

"Yes."

Taffi pounded the large wooden piece against a matching frame, snapping it into place. Liana watched as a completed set piece formed in front of her, a simple dock with a pier leading back to the center of the stage. Before she could acknowledge a job well done, Taffi was already halfway up a ladder to the catwalk above the stage. She watched him unhook a wrinkled backdrop and release it to the bottom of the stage. It had unraveled to reveal an enormous ship with the words *The Drunken Maiden* written on the side. Of course, thought Liana, she had remembered being drawn to this backdrop the day she confronted Stefan. Taffi slid back down on one of the ropes attached to the backdrop.

"Come on," he called. "Give me your hand."

On blind faith alone, Liana stood up and took his hand. They hopped onto the wooden pier and started toward the backdrop of *The Drunken Maiden*. As they got closer, Liana prepped herself to stop, but Taffi kept pulling her forward. Their pace quickened, Liana closed her eyes, and they collided into the backdrop and onto the floor.

"Oww," moaned Liana. They were both in shock but for different reasons.

"It's supposed to work," said Taffi.

"What?" said Liana. "Are we supposed to walk through the backdrop and end up at Hogwarts?"

"Yes," he said pushing his hand up against the image of *The Drunken Maiden*. "I mean no. I must be missing something."

Although exhausted, at least three different jokes, all at the expense of Taffi, had immediately entered her mind. She smiled and looked at him. Taffi, however, was not smiling. In an effort to keep the peace, Liana offered up a suggestion.

"Is it because of your chest?"

Taffi reached up and felt the copper emblem on his chest. "No, it is the object that is magical, not me. It should still work."

Whether conscious or not, Taffi began to pace back and forth just as Liana had done in her bedroom. Normally, Liana would have overanalyzed this as a sign of affection. Mimicry is, after all, the sincerest form of flattery. But because she was nearly delirious from no food or sleep, she simply retreated back to the hilarious jibes about Taffi "missing something" that remained imprisoned in her mind.

After a moment of silence, Taffi stopped. "A bottle, I need a bottle."

Taffi ran across the stage and stopped just short of his father's old room. He ducked underneath the yellow caution tape and disappeared inside. This room, too, was lit only by the red glow of the exit sign above the entryway. Taffi was surprised to see what looked like a war zone: Various props, tools, lumber, and muslin were scattered across the room. Furniture was covered in dust from the settling rubble of the broken brick wall. Between the darkness and the disarray, Taffi could barely make a path toward the back of the room. Making his way through the debris, he found himself surrounded by the crumbled brick that had buried Stefan after he was pushed by Liana. Taffi stood in it for a moment, the evidence of the great and terrible power that he sought to release in Liana. *Was this a good idea? Could he contain her? Did he want to contain her?* The copper emblem on his chest began to hurt, reminding him of what would happen if he didn't release the strength within her. Taffi clutched at his chest and regained his focus.

He approached the large metal cabinet that Stefan had been rummaging through during Liana's last visit. Among the dusty old books sat a typical Middle Eastern lamp and a bottle of champagne. Taffi's eyes lit up—this was what he was looking for. He grabbed the bottle of champagne. It was sticky, as if someone had already popped the cork and allowed its contents to cascade in bubbles down the side, but the cork and wire atop its neck were still in place and intact. He had what he had come for and could have turned to go back to Liana and *The Drunken Maiden*, but something else in the metal cabinet caught his eye. Although there was no light to reflect, something behind the Middle Eastern lamp began to reflect light. Taffi reached in and grabbed a golden lighter with a symbol etched into its side: a loop like the bottom half of the lowercase *g* with some dots trailing above it and to the right. It was strange; he had never seen it there before.

Meanwhile, Liana had wandered down to the holding area in search of Taffy, the horse. She sat in the makeshift stable alongside him, shoving carrots into her mouth. It wasn't her usual breakfast, but this wasn't a usual morning. Just as the daylight had started to peek in the nearby window, a voice rang out.

"Hello? Who's in there?" the voice shouted.

Liana bolted up from her blanket of hay and ran for the stage. "Taffi!" she shouted as she came face to face with the night security guard that stumbled into her the day she confronted Stefan.

"This is private property," he shouted.

"Wait, it's me. Don't you remember you ran into—"

"Show yourself before I call the police," he interrupted as he walked right through her. Liana had again forgotten that she was invisible to other humans. But Taffi wasn't.

"Taffi!" she called. "Someone's coming!"

Taffi heard her from a distance, but it was too late.

"What are you doing here?" said the security guard.

Taffi pocketed the golden lighter just in time to hide it from the glare of the guard's flashlight.

"I can explain," said Taffi, but the security guard heard nothing over the loud mantra that played in his head over and over again: don't die, don't die, don't die. He was, in normal circumstances, a very nice older man. However, after spending his life as an accountant who only ever wanted to be a professional magician but developed tremors three months after retirement, crushing his dream and limiting his access to the world of magic to working as a security guard at his favorite magician's show, he understandably overreacted.

The guard pulled out his gun and pointed it at Taffi.

"Put your hands where I can see them," he shouted.

"Wait!" said Taffi. "My father works here!" He noticed the guard's hands shaking as he pointed the gun toward him.

"Put your hands up!"

Taffi knew the guard's shaking hands and the dark room put him at a great advantage. If the guard did fire a shot, he would almost certainly miss. Taffi reached down for a nearby box of nails and tossed them at the security guard. A shot rang out! Just as Taffi had anticipated, the bullet missed him by at least ten feet. Seizing the opportunity, Taffi ran past the distracted security guard, through the yellow caution tape, and back to the stage. Champagne bottle in hand, Taffi ran toward *The Drunken Maiden* and ceremoniously broke it on the bow of the ship. Glass and champagne sprayed across the stage.

"Liana!" called Taffi, as he frantically looked around.

"Freeze!" said the guard.

Taffi came face to face with him and put up his hands. Tremor or not, he probably wouldn't miss from a twelve-inch distance. Suddenly, a horse's neigh was heard in the distance. Taffy the horse emerged from the back of the stage with Liana on his back. They galloped toward Taffi with a triumphant stride.

"Get on!" she said.

Before the security guard could reconcile the image of the self-tightening reigns on the horse, Taffi had hoisted himself up and they were off.

"Onto the ship!" he said. "Jump onto *The Drunken Maiden*."

The horse reared up, knocking the guard to the floor, and started for the wooden dock.

"No, wait!" Liana pulled back on the reigns, but the horse gained momentum.

"Faster!" said Taffi.

"I'm not ready!"

Her efforts were futile. She closed her eyes and braced herself. The horse jumped up and through the backdrop of *The Drunken Maiden*. Liana opened her eyes and found herself flying above the ocean. Behind her was a real wooden dock littered with fishermen and their accompanying odor. In front of her was the bow of *The Drunken Maiden*, a huge cargo ship docked just a few feet farther than Taffy could jump. Taffy, Liana, and Taffi quickly lost altitude and fell into the ocean.

Chapter *16*

LEAVING FOR GOOD

The wood on the platform, still damp from the early morning mist, bowed slightly with each step of the dainty, naked feet pressing down from above. From the water below, the pier looked alive, as if with each bending plank a breath was taken in and then exhaled. Like an accordion, planks expanded and contracted until reaching the middle of the pier and then suddenly stopped. The breathing had stopped. I stood with my hand outstretched toward Alexander, still grounded in the earth just beyond the dock.

"Are you sure you want to do this?" he said.

"Yes," I said. He knew what my answer would be. It was he who was not sure.

"There's no going back after this," said Alexander.

"I know. It is the only place where we will be safe." Again, Alexander knew this would be my response, but he needed to hear it anyway.

"Okay," he said to himself as he took his first step onto the living pier.

Taking his hand in mine, I escorted Alexander across the pier and onto a very large and ancient-looking ship, across the side of which read: The Drunken Maiden. *Its once golden-brown exterior was now stained a dark earthy green, as if wearing the ocean's seaweed like a heavy sweater to keep warm. Like the planks on the dock, the ship, too, seemed to have a life of its own, like it was watching us, watching him.*

"Well, well, my lady," said the captain, "nice to see you again."

Alexander assumed his place as the lesser species and did not make eye contact with this large, exotic genie. He was more like the stereotypical-looking genie with his long black ponytail and stern dark eyes. He even had the token chiseled physique: a chest so large a child might confuse it with a full-sized mattress. There were, however, no pointy shoes or baggy pants.

"Hello, Captain," I said.

I tried to get past him as quickly as possible. He was rather chatty and would often invite me to join him in some unsavory activity, usually involving some form of intoxication.

"Taking him back?" said the captain.

"Yes."

"I'm sorry he wasn't to your liking."

I stopped and turned toward him. I could have left it there, but in the interest of avoiding any future suspicion, I took a moment to remind the captain of his place. I am after all, a Marid, and if so desired, could reduce the captain from an aesthetic specimen to a whimpering troll.

"It is none of your business what is to my liking or what isn't."

That was all it took. You could almost see the captain's bravado shrink down to size.

"I'm sorry," he said, "I just meant that, if it pleases you, there are many more to choose from. The colonies are ripe with eager, angry young men."

I smiled at him, took Alexander's hand, and walked away. We would not be bothered again.

The captain stood on a platform in the middle of the ship and exhaled a huge wind from his lips. Two large sails, stained with streaks of dirty seawater, unfolded from the tall mast and drunk in the captain's wind. The Drunken Maiden *began to move forward.*

"Next stop," shouted the captain, "the New World."

Chapter 17

THE DRUNKEN MAIDEN

The room was wide, like an empty gymnasium; only instead of polished wooden floors, there was a harsh metal surface. Its geometrically placed nuts and bolts were rusted, not by water, but by the salty, thick haze that relentlessly weighed down on them. Liana awoke to find herself lying, not next to Taffi or Taffy, but among various oddities: a small two-passenger plane, an old Model T car, an Egyptian sarcophagus, and many more museum-like pieces placed randomly around the room. *How did I get here?* The objects around her were so intriguing that the whereabouts of her companions became trivial, even insignificant. Surely this was a dream, or there was some sort of magic at play. Liana moved in awe around the pieces, examining each of them as she passed.

A large table-like stone with ancient writing sat in her path. Next to it was a framed painting of the completed Stonehenge. Its purpose was like that of the accompanying photo next to a coffin, to remind you what the departed once looked like, to remind you of its grandeur. Upon a closer look, Liana recognized the stone before her in the center of the painting as the sacrificial altar of Stonehenge. She retraced her steps backward, hoping to find an exit, but ran into the two-passenger plane. Like the stone altar, it, too, was accompanied by a framed object, an old newspaper dated September 5, 1894. The headline read: "Bermuda Triangle Claims Another Victim." Just below it was a picture of a small two-passenger plane with the name *Sea Hawk* written on it. Before her eyes could confirm it, Liana knew the plane before her would bear the same name, and it did.

Through the dark, salty haze of the room, Liana spotted a dancing reflection of light near the opposite corner. She carefully made her way through the fog to the source of the reflection—a stone basin filled with water and surrounded by flowers. Leaning in for a closer look, Liana knocked over a couple of wooden buckets next to the basin. The sound of wood knocking into metal rang out through the room, but it had no effect on Liana; she only leaned in closer to look in the basin. She picked one of the flowers, smelled it, and placed it back in the water. This one pleasant moment, in the midst of mostly chaotic moments over the past two days, was instantly stolen from her as the flower dried up and turned black. Liana recoiled in fear. Her eyes started to well up with tears. There was laughing in the distance. Was someone laughing at her?

Liana looked in the direction of the laughter and found the

source of the reflecting light: a staircase. Eager to escape this tomb of secret relics, Liana carefully climbed the stairs. The laughter got louder with each step. At the top was a large red curtain, seemingly hung by nothing but thin air. In fact, when looking up Liana couldn't see where it ended or began; it just went on forever. At this point, she wondered if she was dreaming again. Perhaps, when pulling back the curtain, the beautiful woman and Alexander would greet her.

Again the laughter got louder. Could they hear her thoughts? Not knowing what to expect, Liana carefully pulled back a corner of the curtain. She did not see the beautiful woman or Alexander, but it still looked like a dream. It was another large room, this one bathed in red light and covered in red velvet. Small platforms of different sizes and heights were scattered about the room, one of them just behind the curtain. Liana reached out to touch it; she felt the sensation of warm red leather over muscle and fat. Was it alive? Suddenly, a scantily clad couple leapt onto the living platform in front of her. Liana jumped back and closed the curtain. She heard the laughter again. Only this time it sped up and slowed down sporadically, almost like it was being manipulating by a DJ.

Still believing there was a strong possibility this was a dream, Liana pulled back the curtain again and peeked into the room. Through the contorted bodies in front of her, she saw several other scantily clad men and women dancing in and around swirls of multicolored smoke. The movement of the group was rhythmic—sometimes slow then fast—and somehow in tune with the rest of the room and all its inanimate objects. Even animals were present; mostly exotic birds and a couple of tigers. They moved in sync with the others and even chanted or sang along in this scene that begged for music, begged for a climax.

Liana watched each hypnotic movement until she recognized one of the men, the captain. He had the same dark eyes, bare broad chest, and dark ponytail. Now convinced this was a continuation of her previous dream, Liana pulled back the curtain and began to walk forward.

"Stop!" cried a voice from the distance.

A hand shot out from the darkness and pulled Liana behind the curtain. Liana was relieved to discover the owner of the hand.

"Taffi?! Where were you? Where are we? Who are those people?"

"Come with me," he said, ignoring all her questions, as he began to pull her down an adjacent hallway.

"Wait!" said Liana. "I know that man."

"They are genies. We are on *The Drunken Maiden*. I was trying to hide." Without missing a beat, Taffi turned a sharp corner and pulled Liana up another flight of narrow stairs.

"What?" said Liana, "Why? You're a genie, and they can't see me."

Taffi stopped in his tracks, and Liana, like a trailer hitched to a speeding truck, slammed into him, knocking them both to the metal-grated platform beneath their feet. In an awkward moment, Liana found herself lying on top of Taffi. He tried to hold his breath, for fear that it might be rancid after days of no food. "They can see you; humans cannot."

"Oh," Liana softly replied. Sensing the urgency of the matter, she began to get up.

"And I am weak," said Taffi. "They would take advantage of that." He grabbed her hand and began pulling her forward again.

"How did we get here?"

"Magic."

Liana stopped him. "You have your strength back?"

Taffi looked into her eyes. She seemed happy for him. No one had ever felt happy for him.

"I don't know," he said. "When we fell in the water, I felt something, but..." He didn't want to tell her the truth. He had lied so much in his lifetime, what was one more? One more lie to hold onto that feeling of compassion she had given him for the fourth time now. It was coming faster and more frequent than before. *Would it eventually end? Would the lies catch up with him?*

"I don't know if it was me," he said.

"What do you mean?"

Taffi could not weigh all the pros and cons of being honest in that split second, so he instead avoided the subject altogether. "Come on, we have to hurry before we get off course."

He pulled her again toward another staircase, this time going down. They entered a dark room. Across from them, two large camels made of sand guarded a tiny alcove off to the right. To the left was a large metal door. Inside the alcove were several men and women with little clothing held to the ground by the tails of large iguanas clutching the floor.

Liana and Taffi hid behind two large pipes traveling through the first, second, and third decks of the ship.

"What is this place?" said Liana. "Why are those people trapped?"

"Those are slaves."

"What?"

"Genies use this boat to transport human slaves back to their lands. They have been doing it for centuries. The boat has changed over the years, but not its purpose."

"We have to help them."

New to being on the receiving end of compassion, Taffi did not want to give it up or share it with anyone else. *Did she like those humans more than him? Did she like him at all anymore? Was she so fickle that she'd share her compassion with any old human that came along?* Taffi certainly wasn't going to tell the truth now.

"We don't have time," he lied. "We must get through the metal door on the left before the boat passes through the mountains."

"Why?" said Liana, "What's on the other side?"

"The way to the Marid; they don't live in the mountains. We must continue on our own." It wasn't completely false; the Marid did not, in fact, live in the mountains.

"I'm not going until we help those people."

"I told you, we don't have time," he lied again. They had at least another hour before they needed to continue off on their own.

"We can't just leave them here!"

Taffi's face suddenly changed, as if something inside him, something old and bitter, had bubbled up to the surface. Liana belonged to him. How dare she even look at those disgusting slaves, much less want to save them.

"They're only humans!"

Liana stopped and stared at him. "What did you say?"

"I said—"

"If I wasn't the descendant of a Marid, would you say the same about me?"

Taffi immediately knew his answer but did not speak it. Yes, he would have called her a disgusting slave. But then, he never would have known her kindness. In the mere seconds of silence between them, Taffi thought back to his childhood and his people, the Ifrit. How do you undo a centuries-old mantra that was taught to them since birth? It was part of them now, their hatred of humans, built into their souls before they knew they even had a choice. That was what bubbled up inside him. Could he control it? Would he eventually betray Liana?

"I'm sorry," said Taffi, "I'm just trying to help you."

"Then help me free those people," said Liana.

Taffi peered at the sand camels standing guard. "Okay, we'll need some water."

"I saw some in the big room with the plane."

"Great," he said and dashed back toward the stairs.

"Wait," she shouted, "it might not be water, exactly."

Taffi kept moving forward, "I know, it's okay."

"What am I supposed to do?"

"Look at the iguanas and concentrate."

Liana looked at the iguanas; she followed the green scales from the top of their heads to the claws embedded into the cold steel of the boat's floor.

"Concentrate on what?" she said.

But it was too late; Taffi was already up the staircase and out of earshot. She looked again at the big lizards. Their tails were wrapped around the limbs of the humans so tightly that some of their fingers had begun to turn black from the loss of blood circulation. She didn't know if this was the "concentrating" that Taffi meant, but she did feel her urge to save them become stronger.

Almost as quickly as he left, Taffi returned with two buckets of water.

"Are you concentrating?" he said.

"Yes."

"Good. On the count of three, I want you to run up to the lizards, look them in the eye, and say, 'Release.'"

"Okay. What are you going to do?"

"One."

"Wait! I'm not ready!"

"Two."

Liana turned to look at the lizards. "Oh, no."

"Three!"

Liana ran toward the iguanas, Taffi in tow, looked the first one in the eye, and firmly shouted, "Release!"

No sooner did the word escape her mouth than Taffi launched the first bucket of water onto the nearest camel. A deep guttural moan squeezed its way out of the camel's sandy mouth just before its eyes and nose melted over it.

The iguanas had not moved at all.

"It's not working," shouted Liana.

"Concentrate!" said Taffi, as he doused the second camel with the last bucket of water.

"Release!" said Liana.

Still, there was no movement from the iguanas. Both camels' faces melted and hardened as the strange water trickled down their backs. Their limbs flailed about, releasing grains of sand all over the room. Taffi dodged his way past the camels and opened the large metal door to the left.

"Come on!" said Taffi.

"No!" said Liana. "It's not working. I need you to help me!"

"I can't!"

"You said you would!"

The camels began to thump and gallop about the room. Sand started falling off them in piles. Taffi looked down at the lizards and stared as hard as he could.

"Release!" he shouted.

Nothing happened. He didn't want to, but he noticed tears streaming down Liana's face. Suddenly that same feeling of anger bubbled up from inside him; this time it wasn't from hatred bred within him but instead from the thought that Liana was hurting inside. He stood tall, puffed out his chest, and bore down on the iguanas.

"Release!" he said.

The nearest iguana darted his tongue out at Taffi, as if mocking him. Blood began to gather around the copper emblem embedded in Taffi's chest. Liana became desperate, doubling over in emotional pain at the thought of leaving those poor humans trapped. Taffi, too, was doubled over in pain. The strain of trying to use his powers was too much for him. Taffi looked over at Liana. *Was this how it felt?* he thought. While he could not feel what she was feeling, he was still experiencing crippling pain. Was this what heartbreak felt like?

A headless camel knocked Taffi to the ground.

"Taffi!" cried Liana. She helped him up just in time to evade another pass by the headless camels.

"We have to go now!" Taffi said.

"No!" she answered as she ran to the trapped humans. In the back laid a little boy, not much older than six or seven. Liana grabbed the iguana coiled around the boy's wrist and was immediately bitten. The lizard sank his teeth deep into her skin, stopping just short of the bone. Liana screamed in agony. Taffi quickly ran to her aid and pulled her back toward the open door.

"Come on," he said, "we have to go now!"

The little boy looked up at Taffi. *Was he talking to me?* Not knowing whether Taffi was a friend or foe, the boy smiled, painful as it was, and searched frantically within himself for the strength to speak.

"Yes, I want to go with you!" gasped the little boy. "I wish to be set free!"

Taffi looked into the boy's eyes and expected disdain but instead found recognition. All the pain he had felt as a little boy, the pain caused by a seed of hatred planted in him by his father, was there in the boy's eyes. He had been abandoned, too. Taffi was not ready to confront this part of himself, nor did he have the time, as the back half of one of the sand camels was charging toward them like a headless, neckless ostrich. He quickly directed Liana out of harm's way and started again for the metal door.

"No!" pleaded Liana. "Release! Release!"

The other headless camel rounded the corner of the room and started charging for them. Taffi pulled her through the metal doorway with all his strength and slammed the door shut. On the inside, the camel crashed into the closed door, creating a huge sand barricade.

"No!" said Liana. "We have to go back."

Liana and Taffi had fallen back onto the outside deck of the ship. Wind whipped through Liana's hair as *The Drunken Maiden* cut through the ocean.

Taffi stood up. "It's too late," he said as he made his way for a nearby rowboat. Liana, still crying, got up on her knees and pulled on the lever of the big metal door.

"Release!" she tried again.

Taffi untied the rope from the rowboat, sending it crashing into the water below.

"I'm sorry," he shouted, "it's too late. We have to go now!"

"No!"

Taffi grabbed her and pulled her into the rowboat with him. *The Drunken Maiden* sped away from them as they drifted calmly over its wake. She could have struggled, maybe even forced him to stay, but she didn't. She simply curled up in the rowboat, closed her eyes, and in that moment of peace, she whispered, "Set them free."

On the opposite side of that big metal door, the iguanas loosened their grips and let the humans go. And while she didn't know it at the time, Liana had just willingly used her powers.

Chapter 18

THE DRUNK UNCLE

Nothing. Liana sat curled up with her head resting on the edge of the rowboat and felt nothing. As her family life was less than normal, depression often came and went like a drunk uncle, welcome and unwelcome at the same time. People often think they can escape its grasp by changing their environment, but, like a drunk uncle, depression can find you, wherever you end up. And even in the vastness of the ocean, on the tiny speck of a rowboat that floated undetected by any plane flying overhead, depression found its way to Liana. Although horribly debilitating, Liana found it oddly comforting, a familiar feeling in an unfamiliar place. She began to think about her father and what he must be going through as each day passed without knowing where she was or if she was even alive. If only he were here, she thought, he could make the sadness go away like he did so many times when she was a child. Whenever the "episodes" from her mother became too much or too ugly, Jamison would always distract her with a magic trick. It was a gift. He was the only one who could ever pull her out of her depression. Now what would she do without him?

Liana peered into space with a near-catatonic expression. Taffi sat a few feet from her, pulling the oars through and above the water's surface at a deliberate pace. Logically, Liana knew she should be grateful for not having to row, but she still felt nothing. In a small effort to escape her depression, Liana focused on the peaceful cadence of the oars hitting the water. In and out, in and out, in and out...

"Are you hungry?" said Taffi.

He might as well have said nothing, as Liana continued to focus on the methodical beat of the oars: in and out, in and out, in and out.

Again, Taffi inquired, "You must be starving."

This time Liana heard him and decided to let her depression do the talking. "Why didn't you help me?"

Taffi stopped rowing and turned his head. "I did help you."

And so it began. Like so many other drunk uncles at their tipping point, the inevitable "truth" was released from its dormant state, and Liana's depression spewed forth a vomitus rant. "No, you didn't! You got your powers back, and you left those people there to be tortured!"

Taffi did not have a drunk uncle, nor did he know anyone who did, so he was not familiar with the acceptable "drunk uncle" protocol, which clearly states that you should not reply as such.

"You're crazy."

Liana sat up on her knees. "Were you trying to test me or something?"

Still not getting it, Taffi made another unacceptable response. "Calm down."

"Because I'm not a genie! I didn't inherit some gift from any genie ancestor!"

Finally, Taffi caught on, "I'm sorry." He stood up and peered into the water below.

"Now what? Are you going to leave me for dead like you did those other humans?"

Taffi bent his knees slightly and dove into the ocean.

"Wait!" Liana leaned over the edge of the boat. "Taffi! Come back!" There was no trace of him. She surveyed her situation and saw nothing but water.

"Come back!"

Taffi was a quick study. It took most humans countless trials before realizing the only solution to a "drunk uncle" rant is to remove the audience. With no outlet for her anger, Liana's mind began to turn back on her. She sat down and quietly began to panic.

"Taffi!"

"Yes?" his head had emerged from the water just seconds

before Liana's last call. While depression was, indeed, an almost impenetrable human condition, it could still be trumped by one thing: survival. Until, of course, it didn't.

"I'm sorry," said Liana. "Please don't leave me."

Most humans, at this point, would relish victory against the drunk uncle, but Taffi did not. He was many things—deceitful, lazy, mischievous, untrustworthy, and dangerous—but he was not petty. Whether he understood depression or not, he did understand that the human body, like any other living or nonliving vessel, required fuel for optimal performance, and he needed her to be optimal.

"You're hungry," he stated plainly and tossed two fish into the boat.

Liana retreated back into her corner of their tiny temporary home and almost blushed. He was right. She was hungry. Taffi climbed back into the boat and began pulling scales off the fish. Despite his practical, nonemotional interpretation of Liana's behavior, he did feel some guilt. She was right; he could've done more to free those people. As he thought, Taffi's guilt turned into fear. Liana's perception of genies would be shaped by her experiences with them, with him. If he did not keep her as an ally, she could abandon him, or worse, destroy him.

"We're not all like that," said Taffi.

"Like what?"

"The genies on the ship. We are not all like them."

"Really?"

"Really." Taffi completed de-scaling the first fish and moved on to the second. "There are five tribes of genies. You already know of the Marid. There is also the Jann and the Jinn. They are the least powerful. They also have the most contact with humans. They like humans."

"Why haven't I met any of them?" said Liana, as she picked up the first skinned fish and took a bite.

Ignoring her question, Taffi continued, "There are also the Shaitan and the Ifrit. They do not like humans. Those are the genies you saw on the ship."

"They looked like drunken criminals," said Liana with a mouth full of fish. Again, Taffi ignored her comments and began to eat his share.

"The Ifrit are very powerful genies," he said.

"Why do they hate humans?"

Taffi set his half-eaten fish in a small puddle that gathered on the bottom of the boat. His face became sullen and his eyes mirrored those of the little human boy they had left on *The Drunken Maiden*.

"Centuries ago," started Taffi, "the human King Solomon devised powerful methods of enslaving genies. Up until his reign, we had no boundaries and feared nothing. The Ifrit and Shaitan suffered the most loss. Many of my father's friends and family are still trapped in objects hidden around the world."

"But that was so long ago," said Liana as she swallowed her last bite of fish.

"We can live for thousands of years."

Thousands of years, thought Liana, *alone and trapped*. She thought of her mother and her supposed mental illness. Liana knew how devastating it was to know that someone close to you was stuck in an invisible prison with nothing to look at, nothing to hope for, nothing to gain, only the loss of memories as each day passed by.

"You are an Ifrit," said Liana.

"Yes."

"Do you hate humans?"

Taffi looked away and said nothing. For as much as they were different, they were the same. Each of them had witnessed the suffering of a loved one, powerless to stop it, and now feared they would have the same fate. Would she, too, seek revenge, as the Shaitan and Ifrit had? If depression was something tangible, a person that you could reach out and touch, would she grab him? Would she wrap her hands around his neck and squeeze it in the name of…of what? Revenge, love, honor? *Maybe she would.*

Taffi and Liana looked at each other again, for the first time, without judgment. Taffi could see the empathy on her face and felt a kind of validation. His face turned from darkness to light, and he smiled.

"It wasn't me," he said.

"What?"

"I do not have my powers back. I wasn't the one who carried us out of the water and onto the ship."

"Then who did?"

Taffi looked at her and raised his eyebrows, "You."

Chapter **19**

LIVING AMONG THE SLAVES

A man, dressed in colonial garb complete with a tricorn hat, pulled gently back on the reins, bringing his carriage to a halt. In front of him crossed a woman and child, each with checkered aprons and baskets of fabric. As their feet, covered in black leather shoes with a slight heel and worn brass buckles, reached the edge of the dirt road, the carriage driver gave the signal, and the horses moved on. The wheels, large enough to be the bones of someone's modern-day repurposed coffee table, rolled by a modest house. Its white shutters contrasted the gray exterior as they should but remained closed. Closed shutters were odd this time of year. If one was so inclined, he might stop and peer through the wooden slats to see what was hiding in this modest gray house. And if he did, he would see me sitting in a chair behind a wooden table. On my head, a white-laced bonnet tried to contain the dark locks of my hair as they haphazardly poked out in search of freedom. My face, covered in the shadows, wanted to come out, wanted to be seen, but was forced to stay back and stay hidden. I was now nearly unrecognizable to those who knew me before. A bulky frock that imprisoned my best assets replaced my form-fitting white wrap.

I was alone, and like Liana in that small rowboat, I was hungry.

The window toward the back of the modest house was open and overlooked a small field with wandering livestock. A brown-and-white cow shuffled by the window and then stopped for a moment to chew its cud. Could cows not chew cud and walk at the same time? I looked toward the front of the house, looked back at the cow, and closed my eyes. A small flash of light, almost like a blue lightning bolt, shone briefly where the cow stood. I opened my eyes and watched a perfectly cut slab of beef levitate through the open window, into the house, and onto a cast-iron pan on a nearby stove. As it started to cook, I heard the front door begin to open. I quickly positioned myself in front of the stove as if I had done something wrong.

"I'm ready!" said Alexander. He entered the modest house dressed as a stereotypical Native American Indian. Relieved, I leaned back in my chair to reveal the cooking meat.

"What are you doing?" he said.

"I'm hungry."

"But we just ate twenty minutes ago."

"I can't help it. It's the baby."

Not happy, but not terribly upset either, Alexander shuffled over to the back open window in his leathery, feathered outfit.

"Did anyone see you?" he said.

"No."

"Are you sure?"

"Yes!" I wasn't really sure, but seeing as my new town had fewer people than a fly has eyes, the odds were in my favor.

"This is the seventh time you've eaten today," said Alexander, "and I'm not talking about snacks."

Like Taffi's in the rowboat, my face became sullen and dark as I retreated back to the shadows of the room. "I'm not like the other women here."

Alexander stopped in his tracks and looked down in shame. We had been through this before, many times. The comforts of his own land and his own people made it easy to forget that I was different. Many times, he was in my world with my people, and the discomforts and unfamiliarity would weigh down on him so much that our love almost wasn't enough.

"You're right," he said, "I'm sorry."

I accepted his apology with a smile.

"Can I get you anything?" he said.

"No, I'm fine."

"Are you sure?"

"Yes."

Alexander walked over to me and gently kissed my head.

"I won't be long," he said.

Suddenly concerned, I sat upright, "If any of those British humans lay a finger on you—"

"I know. You'll eat them."

I smiled. "No, no, the English are too bland."

We both laughed. Alexander rushed back to kiss me one more time and then darted out into the street.

I sat still for a moment and looked around. Despite my modest living conditions and my modest human life, I was happy.

"Is this what you've been reduced to?" said a disembodied voice from afar. I looked to my left and saw Stefan standing in the corner. He was as creepy, dark, and ominous as I had remembered.

"You're not welcome here," I said.

"I've come to take you home," he said, dismissing me like he had so many times with all the women in his life. I was, after all, just a woman.

"You're wasting your time," I said.

Stefan walked over to the stove and picked up the sizzling cast-iron pan and its accompanying porterhouse steak. "Is this really what you want?"

I said nothing. Stefan, fluffing his "peacock" feathers, waved his hand over the stove to put out the fire and then tossed the steak over to the wooden table standing in front of me. As it soared through the weightless specks of dust made visible only by the light of the sunset shining through the back window, it took on a different shape—bigger, thicker, and more colorful. The steak landed in front of me, only now it was a fully cooked Cornish hen with stuffing and all the trimmings. I was not impressed and *simply pushed the plate of food away.*

As one may guess, winning the affections of a woman was not in Stefan's repertoire. It was a delicate art of confidence combined with humility and thoughtfulness that he never quite mastered, nor cared to. Viewing a woman as a piece of property was a much easier way to get what he wanted. Until, of course, he had met his match. Though he hated that he could not control me, that uncertainty was often the very thing that made him covet me.

"Enough of this!" Stefan said. "You're a Marid. You could crush this entire house with a thought. Instead you stifle yourself, looking over your shoulder at every moment, afraid that if anyone sees your strengths they'll burn you at the stake. As if they could."

"I'm not going back with you," I stated plainly.

"It's okay. I forgive you. We all like to have fun with humans. No one will begrudge you for that. We can still get married. We can still unite our families."

I was indifferent about his presence before but was now becoming angry. "I told you, I'm not marrying you."

Stefan stopped and bore down on me sternly. Forgiving me had no effect, so now he would try insults. "I knew your word meant nothing. You'd rather be with a slave, one that dresses up like a savage to go throw boxes of tea off a boat."

"He stands for something," I shouted.

"Something you already have."

I could feel a temper building inside me. Is this what he wanted? Anger is bad for the baby. Does he know I'm pregnant? He couldn't know. I struggled to find the words to calm my spirit.

"I love him!"

"You're drunk on the idea of human love," said Stefan.

Am I? My father had said the same thing to me before I left. Why does everyone keep saying that? Was this all a mistake? My mind began to race. Were they right? Am I just hungry? What was happening to me? Maybe it was the pregnancy? And then I suddenly became calm. The pregnancy. I wasn't drunk or wrong or hungry—well, maybe a little hungry—I was pregnant. And that proved that my union with a human was more than just fun or a mistake. Many genies had been with humans, but none of them had ever become pregnant, until now, until me.

"You're wrong," I said and stood up proudly to reveal my pregnant belly.

"No!" said Stefan. His eyes widened and bulged out of their sockets like the distended bellies of malnourished children. "This is a disgrace!"

Stefan's entire life, entire identity, was built upon the notion that humans were lesser beings, a step backward—the idea that no matter how terrible, useless, or insignificant he became, he would always be better than a human. His status, confidence, and existence depended on it. And now, the very woman whom he had stepped on so many humans to reach had pulled one of them out from under him. What was he without the idea of human inferiority to lift him up? In this one moment, the mighty fortress he had built upon for so many years with bricks of anger, revenge, and purpose was breached without a single fight, life lost, or spell cast. All by one woman, unfettered by the scars of my people, and my capacity to love.

Backed into a corner of his own creation, Stefan began to act out. A wave of his left hand sent the Cornish hen he had so proudly made crashing into the wall above the stove. "You have defiled your kind!" he said. "Even the Marid will not forgive you for this!"

"You're wrong," I said. My confidence only angered him more.

He waved his other hand, sending the wooden table across the room to crash into the opposite wall. "You have no right to speak!"

I had had enough. I raised my right hand, sending Stefan into the wall behind him with the force of a hurricane wind. The wooden beams of the modest house splintered and cracked under the weight of my strength.

"Do not test me, Stefan."

He tried to move but could not. If he could have cried, if he could have begged, he would have, but even as he lay paralyzed against the wall, without ever knowing forgiveness or kindness or humility, he could only draw upon the one emotion he was ever taught or shown: anger. And in the interest of survival, he drew upon that emotion now more than ever. Now I was the object of his anger. I was as disgusting and pathetic as a human. How else would he justify my actions? That was the only explanation. He looked upon me with generations of disgust; his family, his friends still trapped by King Solomon's magic, they would all look to me now. I had become the proxy for all human kind, and the Ifrit could be avenged only by destroying my human husband, our disgusting spawn, and me.

"I do not wish to see you again," I said.

Smoke began to rise up and around Stefan's feet, spinning around his legs like a mini tornado.

"Get used to these slaves you live amongst," he said. "Soon you will be one of them."

I stared at him without fear. There was a part of me that felt sorry for him, Genies were not born with hatred; it was forced into them.

"Goodbye, Stefan."

The smoke tornado grew around Stefan and then fell to the ground to reveal an empty space.

Chapter *20*

NOT A VOLCANO

Liana floated in a semi-conscious state where she was not asleep but not yet awake. Our last dream lingered in her mind, leaving her to wake with a feeling of sorrow, a feeling of sadness for Stefan. She tried to fall back into the dream, to illicit some other emotion, anything but compassion for Stefan, but the rising sun kept drawing her out, back to reality, back to the rowboat. She finally gave in, opened her eyes, and found Taffi sitting in the same spot she'd left him in, methodically rowing the boat. He noticed Liana stirring behind him and glanced back with a smile.

"Sleep well?" he said.

"Yes," she replied as she stretched out her arms to accompany her lion-like yawn.

"Good," said Taffi, "we're almost there."

Liana raised her eyebrows thoughtfully. Perhaps if she transferred this lingering feeling of compassion for Stefan onto Taffi, she could move on with her day without feeling like she'd just kissed the devil. Although would kissing the devil's son be any better? Taffi was so different from his father. *Or was he?*

"Is your father married?" said Liana.

Taffi glanced back at her, grateful for the conversation but disappointed by the topic. "Yes, to my mother."

His mother, thought Liana, how wonderful! Perhaps Stefan wasn't made of pure hatred after all. And that would explain Taffi's kindness—he must have learned it from his mother. But where was she now? And why did she not appear in Liana's dreams? Was she dead? Or trapped? This new information flooded Liana's head with a million questions.

"Is she still…?"

"Yes," interrupted Taffi, "she lives with her family."

He turned away from her. His body grew rigid as his rowing pace quickened. Liana sensed the tension in his voice and body language but still probed on.

"She doesn't live with your father?" she said.

"They do not love each other. They were married only out of necessity."

Liana's face and body language now matched his. Her mind had so quickly painted a picture of a Stefan who, although rough and dark on the exterior, might still have goodness in his heart. But now that picture was overexposed, and the light within it exploded and turned to darkness.

"Necessity?" she said.

"Yes. My father refused to marry anyone for several years."

"Why?"

Taffi finally turned to face her. His eyes were vacant, like those of an abused child whose soul was extinguished as an ember, never knowing the nourishment of oxygen or the kindling it needed to blossom into a full flame. His eyelids laid heavy over his pupils, trying to contain his sadness and guilt. Genies, like humans, typically didn't like to open up old wounds and relive the feeling of fresh raw pain, but they were almost to the Marid, and Taffi needed Liana on his side. She would be the only one standing between him and the wrath of her ancestors.

"My father was betrothed to one of the Marid," he said, "but they never got married."

It seemed that Liana's dreams had finally caught up with reality. Excitement ran up her spine, straightening her back as it traveled down to her hips and feet. If Taffi knew about Stefan and the woman in her dreams, perhaps he knew where she was—*where I was.*

"What happened to her?" she said.

Taffi turned away from her again. "She was killed."

Liana's posture went limp. Like Taffi, her eyes had now become vacant and her lids tried to contain the pooling moisture within them.

"Killed?" she said softly.

"Their union was supposed to unite the Marid and the Ifrit," said Taffi. "Many did not want this. It is suspected she was killed for this reason."

Liana knew that was not the reason. She wondered how many genies knew the truth about Stefan and the woman in her dreams. It was no surprise that he would keep it from his son, but how many others knew of the bastard child? How solid was the line between dignity and revenge? Surely Stefan couldn't have defeated her alone. She was far stronger than him in her dreams; he must have had help from other Ifrit. And what about the Marid? Did they know?

Though Taffi could not see her, he sensed a single tear streaming down from one of Liana's eyes. He began to think that his decision to "show and tell" had backfired on him. His effort to cement an essential ally may have instead planted the seeds of revenge, and he was the first Ifrit in her path. Taffi spotted a large volcano ahead in the distance and knew he had to act fast. Perhaps if he shifted the focus back to his mother, Liana would feel sorry for him again.

"After many years of solitude, my father decided he did not want his bloodline to die. So he chose my mother."

Taffi turned back to gauge Liana's interest. She didn't seem to care.

"She was so innocent and pretty," he spoke up.

Liana turned toward him. "Was?"

Adding a dramatic flair, Taffi turned away again. "My father has hardened her."

While his feigned sadness was born mostly of his instinct to survive, Taffi did still feel grief for his mother. She was, in fact, once pretty and innocent. And if it weren't for those few years during his childhood, when she was still happy and hopeful, he may have never learned kindness, only hatred and revenge from his father. Liana was no dummy. While she could plainly see Taffi's desperate act as it played out in front of her, she could still detect the small bit of real grief underneath his charade. And, as depression begets more depression, a new picture began to form in her mind, one of a young female genie with hopes of meeting her handsome young counterpart. She imagined a shy girl, unnoticed but for her trusting face and contagious smile. Those who had known her when she was young would remember a wild imagination and her ability to find the fun in almost any situation. As she entered adulthood, she set her sights on Stefan, the proud and powerful leader of their tribe. While she was never able to gain his affection, she could always get him to laugh. Year after year, she would fill him up with joy, giving so much of herself, only to be forgotten moments later. Forgotten to objects, ideas, sights, *anything that reminded him of me*. Until one day, when Stefan stormed into her house with so much anger and rage and swept her off her feet. At the time, she mistook the rage for passion, a passion that lay dormant for years, bubbling under the surface, until he finally realized she was his true love, and that passion erupted with great force. And like Alexander and I, a child was born out of this passion: Taffi. Ignored by Stefan, dismissed as a mere vessel to continue his bloodline, this shy genie turned, not to anger or revenge, but to love—love for her son. Consumed with the idea of Taffi's mother, whether it be real or not, Liana looked on him again with compassion. She wondered what it would feel like to know you were spawned out of hate, created through an act of vengeance. She wanted to say something, anything that would replace this terrible thought, but all that came out was, "Look, a volcano."

Taffi had stopped rowing and gazed tentatively at the large volcano as they got closer and closer. Liana saw billows of smoke pouring out of its top.

"That's not a volcano," said Taffi.

Liana examined it again. "That's what it looks like."

Taffi pulled the oars into the boat, as if bracing for some kind of terrible impact.

"Look up," he said.

She did just that, and high above the clouds of smoke, a figure started to take shape. A huge bulbous shoulder pushed the smoke and shifted to reveal a large muscular chest. Before the rest of the figure's torso took shape, a pair of disembodied dark eyes peered down at Taffi and Liana in their tiny rowboat.

Liana's mouth dropped in terror. "Oh my…"

"Hold on!" said Taffi as he grabbed Liana and clung to the bottom of the boat.

A waterspout rose out of the ocean and funneled up to the clouds overhead. Liana closed her eyes and felt herself turning over and over until the ocean water slapped against her skin. As the shock of the cold waves forced her eyes open, she found herself floating alone just a few feet from the capsized boat. Taffi was nowhere in sight. Thunder and lightning filled the sky above as it unleashed a mix of hail and stinging rain.

Liana began to panic. "Help!"

"Grab onto the boat!" said Taffi.

Liana searched but couldn't see him. "Where are you!" Hail pelted her face and shoulders.

"Get to the boat!"

Through the stinging rain, Liana swam with all the energy she could muster until she reached the inverted rowboat. There, she found Taffi. His blood oozed from the copper emblem on his chest faster than ever before. As the rain became thicker and the hail grew larger, sharks began to circle beneath them, attracted by the blood from Taffi's chest. He reached over and grabbed Liana by the shoulder.

"Look at him!" he said.

Liana could barely hear through the howling wind and rapid-fire impact of the hail. "What?!"

"Look at the genie!"

Before Liana could act, the giant genie overhead waved his hand and another waterspout funneled up from the ocean, ripping the rowboat to shreds. Liana and Taffi were thrown apart from each other.

"Help me!" said Liana, barely keeping herself above water.

"Look him in the eyes!" Taffi was again nowhere to be seen.

A huge hand-like wave rose from the ocean and slammed into Liana, pushing her under the water. She closed her eyes again and felt herself turning over and over as the pressure in her head got tighter and tighter. She didn't know which way was up or how deep she was sinking; she knew only that she was helpless, helpless to stop or change anything. How foolish was she to think herself worthy of the terrible gift that forced itself into her life. She was a fraud. A charlatan. Like a toddler with a handgun, she had so much power but no sense of it. She had not earned it. Without someone to guide the gun in her hand, whether it be her mother, her friend Rachel, her cheating ex-boyfriend, Taffi, or her father, she would only misfire and fail. This whole time she had been telling herself that it was Jamison who needed her, when in fact, it was she who needed Jamison. She was so willing to surrender, to just sink, as if that was the safer choice, easier than trying.

A hand reached down searching for something to grab, anything—another hand, a foot, hair, a piece of clothing. Finally, it grabbed ahold of Liana's shirt and pulled upward. Liana rose out of the ocean gasping for breath. Through her tears, she found Taffi treading in front of her and grabbed onto him tightly.

"You have to look him in the eyes," he said.

"I can't."

"Just do it!"

Before she could answer, another hand-like wave plunged them into the water. Again, Liana turned over and over, but this time she kept her eyes open. Still, she could not see anything. The water had darkened from Taffi's blood as it spread across her face and body like some kind of parasitic ghost. He must be close by, she thought, and reached out in every direction hoping her hands would find him. Finally, she felt something; it was cold and rigid, like a slimy skeleton bone. As the last few orbs of oxygen pushed their way through her nose, Liana unconsciously grabbed the slippery thing and frantically made her way back to the surface. She wiped the stinging salt water from her eyes and saw Taffi in front of her. It was him. His body had begun to shrivel like a grape in the sun. Before she could say or do anything, a third waterspout rose up out of the ocean and carried Taffi with it.

"Taffi!" Her eyes followed him up into the sky until he disappeared. "Taffi!" Liana searched the skies looking for any trace of him and found the dark eyes atop the clouded figure above the volcano peering down at her. She suddenly felt a searing pain in her left eye and screamed. She turned away and closed it tightly. She tried to wipe away the pain but only succeeded in making it worse as she splashed salt water onto her face. There was more blood now, but not from Taffi, from her. Her eye was bleeding—the blue contact lens within it had been burned away.

"Taffi! Help me!" Her cries were futile. She was alone and only wanted to die quickly now. Her hands and feet had stopped treading water, and she began to sink. As her chin and forehead sunk beneath the surface, she looked up one last time through the water. Her eyes met with the ominous genie's before she disappeared into the ocean.

She was gone. The waterspouts fell back to the ocean, and the rain stopped. A lone seagull glided over the giant genie and flew down to the surface of the water until it came upon a bright green light beaming from beneath the ocean. It slowly became brighter and brighter. Just a few feet from the surface, Liana floated calmly, as if frozen in time, looking up with her one green eye. It shined like a lighthouse up through the water and into the eyes of the great-clouded genie overhead. The sun began to cut through the crevasses of smoke and cloud, and the genie slowly disappeared back through the mouth of the volcano. Liana's eyes finally found peace and closed gently as she sank farther into the ocean. Slowly, an entourage of sea life came to her side. Fish of all colors and sizes formed a brigade around her and made way for a giant majestic stingray. Liana fell onto the stingray's back like it was a soft mattress, and it carried her toward the surface and onto the shore. It was a royal procession for the return of an heiress.

Chapter 21

AMON

Liana awoke to find herself atop a cliff that jutted out into the sky. Her original clothes were gone, except for my prison still wrapped tightly around her ankle, and she was wrapped in a white, semitransparent garment. Her abdomen was exposed only for a necklace-like belt adorned with various jewels and beads. Liana's hair was braided in segments, once across her forehead and again across the back of her head and down to her shoulders. The jagged rock below her had pushed its way out so far over the ocean that it seemed like she was flying above the surface and into the horizon. A seagull floated in the headwinds beside her, as if they were flying together above the clouds and across the sea. It was all so beautiful, so majestic, so free, that all the questions in her head—Was she alive? How did she get there? Where was Taffi?—seemed unimportant. Though she was far from her purple bed back in that suburban neighborhood, Liana felt like she was home. There was something so familiar about this particular cliff, jutting out above this particular ocean like it was intruding onto the landscape. *Had she been there before?* She knew consciously that she had not, but maybe unconsciously, maybe in her dreams? *Was this the same cliff where the genie and the human talked about confessing their love to her father?*

"You look just like her."

Liana turned and looked behind her. Sunlight swept across her face and body so brightly that she could barely make out a figure standing before her through the glimmering rays. This figure was not ominous and muscular like the one above the volcano but rather plump and tired-looking. One shoulder slumped forward as the other pulled back trying to compensate for its wounded counterpart. His doughy inner thighs met each other just above the knees and stuck together as if propping each other up. He was dressed all in white, and although the material contained no jewels or other reflective ornaments, it seemed to sparkle as he stood, like a thousand tiny paparazzi were snapping pictures. A masculine hand snuck out of the sunlight and gently glided down Liana's cheek. She was at the same time pleased and alarmed. Although the hand seemed young, Liana could tell that if it weren't for the extra fat, it would be wrinkled and covered in creases like a deflated gum bubble. Still, it felt natural, like her father's.

Her father, she had to get back to her father!

"Who are you?!" she said. "Where are my clothes? Where is Taffi?"

All those questions that had seemed so insignificant just moments ago rushed back into her head like an ice cream–induced brain freeze. She stood up, trying to make out the stranger's face, but the sunlight only grew brighter.

"Please, don't be alarmed," he said. "Taffi is safe, and your clothes have been discarded."

The elderly figure finally came out of the light. His face was round and silly, like that of an overweight elf. His hair and eyebrows were as expected, plain and white, but his eyes, they were different; one green and one blue, they peered out from behind his puffy cheeks and looked down at Liana with great joy.

"I am your great-great-great-great-great-great grandfather," he said.

Liana stepped back. "What?"

"You may call me Amon," he said still smiling from ear to ear.

Liana looked him up and down, circling him like a predator stalking its prey. He did look familiar, like...

"The woman in my dreams," she said, "is she...?"

"My daughter? Yes."

Although she was happy, Liana began to inexplicably panic. "Is she here?"

"No."

"Stefan, he did something to her. He cursed me. I need your

help!"

Amon tried to comfort her with his touch, but Liana's mania sent her pacing too fast for him to catch her.

"Calm down, Liana," he said, "you are safe now."

Calm down, she thought. How could she calm down? The events that had transpired over the last twenty-four hours were so unbelievably chaotic and stressful that a medically induced coma would not be able to calm her down.

"No!" she said. "I can't calm down. My father can't see me. He needs me. I've risked my life to come here. You have to help me. Please! I need to trap Stefan; it's the only way."

Amon continued to just stare and smile at her, as if witnessing his child take her first step or speak her first word.

"I will help you," he said.

"Good! There is no time; we have to go now!"

Again, Amon just smiled at her. She was so adorable, he thought.

"Time does not confine us as it does humans," he said as he opened his arms to her. "Come with me; you must be hungry."

As if she had a choice, Liana followed him away from the cliff and into the mouth of a glittering cave. As she walked, her white garment flowed in the wind behind her, and she suddenly didn't look so helpless. She glided across the top of the cliff with fierce intention and alluring beauty. Although it appeared as such from the outside, inside Liana was simply manic and well rested. Even so, she finally looked the part of the powerful half-genie heiress to the Marid. All she needed to do now was believe it.

Like the doomed camels on *The Drunken Maiden*, the cave seemed to be made of sand. Tiny hermit crabs crawled all over the walls, digging in and out as Amon and Liana walked by. Finally, Amon stopped just short of a large sand table covered with bowls of various exotic fruits and vegetables: seaweed, plantains, kale, mango, guava, oranges, coconut, spinach, and artichoke. A silly smile still on his face, Amon stretched out his arm toward the food.

"Please, sit."

Liana was hungry. She hadn't eaten since Taffi had given her a fish in the rowboat, and that was a small fish. Taffi had known she was hungry then, too. *How could they tell?*

Without resistance, Liana sat at the table and began eating. Amon just continued to look at her. Occasionally, Liana would look up at him and he would turn away, but Liana knew he was staring at her. It was odd at first, but by the time she got to her third plantain, it became funny, like some silly game she and Jamison might play at the dinner table. Finally, Liana moved fast enough to make eye contact with him.

"I'm sorry," he said, "I don't mean to stare, it's just that you

144

look so much like my daughter."

Liana wiped the fruit juices off her face and pushed the food away. Although it was obvious Amon was happy to see her, she started to wonder how he really felt about his daughter's bastard child from so many years ago. He had never appeared in her dreams; why? "I thought genies weren't supposed to have children with humans."

Amon knew this was going to be a difficult conversation and thought he should sit down. "They're not," he said as he lowered his malleable thighs onto a sand stool, "In fact, it's almost impossible."

"Then I'm not—"

"You are. Your great-great-great-great grandmother was born out of true love. She was my granddaughter. Only true love between a human and a genie will allow a mixed child to be born. Many genies do not know this. In fact, it is only a legend among our kind."

Liana stood up with confidence and stared down at Amon. How dare he, she thought. How dare he push away his own daughter, especially one capable of loving so deeply that it allowed her to transcend her origins to create something new? She remembered the dream where I was laid up in that modest house in the Colonies, the New World. It wasn't just a new world for the British settlers; it was a new world for genies, too—one full of hope and love instead of fear and hate. Liana felt inspired and powerful as a rush of wind carried the back of her garment up like a hero's cape.

"How could you be ashamed of that?" she said with confidence.

Amon looked at her with that same silly smile. "I'm not."

"Your daughter left to spare you any embarrassment," said Liana, holding her ground as if preparing for a fight.

"She left because of her own embarrassment."

Unable to think of any respectable counterpoint, Liana responded like a four-year-old.

"Liar."

Amon's smile widened, "You are just like her, fighting even after you've won."

Feeling confident with the toddler approach, Liana again threw out the first thought that came into her head. "What's that supposed to mean?"

As Amon knew he was in for a rather difficult exchange, he pivoted his torso and strategically squeezed both thighs together to form one large pillar of strength to hoist his rotund body onto. After a deep breath, he rose to his feet and looked at Liana frankly.

"My dear, if I were ashamed of my daughter, you would be dead."

This comment literally took the wind out of her sails, as her garment fell back to the ground just behind her heels. Amon waved his hand across the table and the various bowls of exotic fruits and vegetables disappeared into a heap of sand, like it was all just a mirage. Liana fell back onto her sandy stool. Now she was the one sitting as Amon looked down at her with confidence. For all the times Liana had wished he would stop looking at her with that silly smile, she wished he would look upon her with it now. She had forgotten herself for a moment. This was not her father's house, and he was not her father. Liana had seen what the beautiful woman was capable of in her dreams and could only imagine what her father could do.

Amon had played this game for years, centuries in fact. His portly, unassuming appearance and accompanying silly smile had welcomed in the overconfident, overbearing, and immature, time and time again, only to be blindsided by his strength, wisdom, and humility. Mostly those who came to him with the anger and vengeance of the past behaved this way. He never punished or tortured them like the Ifrit did. Instead, Amon used reason and compassion to teach, deploying them like soldiers on the battlefield at just the right time and just the right moment. Liana was angry, and she wanted vengeance. Amon knew what had to come next— the silly smile. Perhaps just a smirk would do.

Liana peeked out of the corner of her one green eye and saw the left side of Amon's lips curve up toward the sky. His eyes became softer, as if welcoming in the sun again. She suddenly felt relieved, as if her father had told her she could come out of the naughty spot. Desperate to fill the silence, Liana asked what had been burning in her mind for days.

"What happened to her?"

"Stefan claims she is dead, but I do not believe him. For all his faults, he did still love her, as much as he could love anyone."

This much, Liana knew. He still had not answered her question.

"Then where is she?"

For the first time, Amon looked sad as he spoke, "No one knows. She left us before her child was born and never returned."

The fleshy pillar beneath him opened up and lowered him back onto a nearby stool. Though he did not want to admit it, with all his strength and power, he could not help his daughter.

"Didn't you try to find her?" said Liana.

"She did not want to be found."

Liana wondered for a moment—although she did not yet understand all the "cans" and "cannots" of genie powers, she did recall Stefan barging in on Amon's daughter when she was in the modest colonial house. Certainly she wouldn't have invited him there—*I didn't*—or even told him where she was going. How did he know where to find her?

"Stefan found her," she said.

Amon snapped his neck in her direction, as if waking up from a deep trance.

"What?"

A little startled and oddly excited, Liana replied, "I saw it in a dream, I…"

As the words came out of her mouth, she immediately realized that, although historically pretty accurate, her dreams did not necessarily translate into reality. Amon, however, was stuck on the idea that Stefan had found his daughter. That's impossible, he thought. Before Liana could continue, Amon's fleshy thighs slapped back together as he sprung to his feet. He paced back and forth, not in the traditional straight line, but instead in a zigzag-like fashion across the room.

"The only way he could've found her is if—" Amon suddenly stopped and turned toward Liana again. "Does Taffi know this?"

"I don't know. Why don't you ask him?"

"Because I'm asking you."

Amon did not want to see, smell, hear, or imagine Taffi in any way, much less ask him questions. For all his strength and wisdom, Amon needed an outlet like everybody else, genie or human. He needed a scapegoat, a patsy, somewhere to put all the pain centuries of regret had caused him. Butting heads with Stefan would only cause more war, which Amon did not want; thus, Taffi had become the unlucky target for his anger. And while he was the unofficial master of all things genie, even he could not disguise his hatred of Taffi. Liana felt it, too, like the radiating heat from an angry tiger's slow, deliberate breath. Why did Amon hate Taffi? she wondered. After all that he had done for her, for the Marid. Amon might never have met the heiress of his daughter if it weren't for Taffi. How could he still hate him? No, how dare he? Amon squinted and looked intently into her eyes, as if probing her mind for answers. But Liana didn't want to answer him. She didn't want to back down.

"Where is Taffi? I want to see him."

Amon felt something in her. Liana felt it, too, like the time she pushed Stefan into that brick wall at the theater. It was a feeling of clarity, of purpose and determination. Amon knew this side of her all too well, and if he couldn't contain it, he could lose her just as he had lost his daughter. He pulled back and attempted to speak to Liana's human side.

"You cannot trust him, Liana. He is an Ifrit and the son of Stefan."

Still defiant, Liana fought back.

"He's not like him!"

The feeling inside her grew, and she liked it. It was somehow stronger and more potent than before. Was it this place? The tiny hermit crabs crawling on the sand walls began to line up, one by one, and march toward Amon. An overconfident genie would have sent them back into the sand as a show of dominance, but Amon let them come.

"He's exactly like Stefan."

"No," said Liana, "he's the reason I'm here."

The room began to shake and particles of sand fell from the ceiling, but Amon remained steadfast, carefully choosing each word, each facial tick.

"Do you know what it means to be an Ifrit?" he said.

Liana felt him pulling back, but this incited her only to push further. She could feel her confidence as if it were flowing through her veins. The hermit crabs began to crawl up Amon's feet and legs. The terrain was treacherous, but each hermit crab marched on, past the slippery valley between his thighs, up and over the steep incline of his rotund stomach, and across the thorn-like stubble on his cheeks.

"Yes, I do know what it means to be an Ifrit," she said.

Amon peered through the tiny legs of a hermit crab latched onto his eyelashes and looked into Liana's eyes. "Then why do you trust him? Since your mother went away, you've trusted no one, yet you trust him now."

He was right, thought Liana. Her well of confidence had suddenly sprung a leak, and she began again to doubt herself. The hermit crabs slowly crawled back to the ground. Liana's eyes became heavy and looked off thoughtfully in a different direction. Why did she trust him?

"He saved my life," she said as if finally remembering the answer to some tricky riddle.

The hermit crabs one by one began marching back toward the sand walls as they reached the ground. Amon had found a way in, and although for decades he had wanted his heiress to return and claim her place as a genie of the Marid, he needed to pull her back to the human world, if only just for a moment.

"No," he said, "Taffi made you trust him, like the Ifrit do with all humans. It is a magic that only the Ifrit possess. That is why they are so dangerous. For years, their calculated whispers into the ears of confused men have caused war, fire, famine, and disease. He is using you to get to us, to me."

Liana searched her mind for a counterpoint but could not find one. There was so much she didn't know. If she were still a fool who trusted everyone who smiled at her, that would be something, a reason to explain her trust in Taffi. But she wasn't a fool, not anymore. It didn't make sense. How had she not thought of this before? Taffi had the motive and the power. The power!

"You're wrong!" she said, "Taffi doesn't have his powers. Stefan punished him for helping me!"

Amon looked at her as if searching for a crack in the foundation of the lie that leapt so easily from her lips. But there was no crack; Liana smiled brightly and confidently. She had to, for if she didn't believe it, she might never trust anyone again.

"Stefan punished him?" he said, trying again to detect any hint of deceit.

She wanted to respond as a tween might when winning over her assuming parents, with a smirk, a raise of the eyebrows, a tilt of the head, hands behind her back, and a small sway as if to say, "I told you so." However, still unsure of herself, all she could manage was a raise of the eyebrows and a "See for yourself."

Amon leaned toward her with his silly smile and, like wind blowing away a sand castle, disappeared into the air.

Chapter **22**

REGRET

Liana wanted to go with him, to protect Taffi, or at least hear what they would say to each other, but not only did she not know where Amon was going, but she had no idea how he was getting there. Liana couldn't follow Amon, but I could. I had learned to reach far beyond my prison nearly a century ago. I, too, wanted to know what they would say to each other: two mortal enemies face to face after centuries of stewing. And so, I stretched out my thoughts and followed Amon through the salty air as it carried him toward the ocean and plunged him into the sea.

It felt warm and slippery, like a dog's tongue. His arms and legs could move about freely within this jam-like substance, but they could not penetrate the exterior. Taffi's foot made it all the way to the outermost layer but only poked into it like a mallet pushing down onto the head of a drum. His head was the only body part that breached his mucus-like prison. The walls surrounding him varied in size and shape, all in a deep burgundy color with a glossy finish. As Taffi's eyes slowly adjusted to the dimly lit space, he realized it was not a glossy finish but rather a thin layer of what could only be described as slime covering the walls. Above him was a dark, empty corridor that extended upward into the sky, and below him, just a few feet down a small slope, was a large, fleshy valve. Seemingly the only way out, Taffi gazed at this disgusting valve that lay before him. How could he get to it? Where would it lead? The valve began to move. It pulsed up and down as if preparing for some grand vomitus episode, only to disappoint with the anticlimactic entrance of a head, a pudgy round head. The rest of Amon's body emerged from the valve, and although it only got slimier, Amon somehow did not.

This was perhaps the worst-case scenario Taffi could have imagined: being trapped in a mound of mucus by his father's mortal enemy, while his only possible ally, Liana, was nowhere in sight.

"I come in peace!" he said. "I brought you one of your own."

"Silence," said Amon. He waved his hand, causing the mound of mucus to swell up over Taffi's mouth. Taffi was attempting to extend an olive branch, but in this case, he would've needed an olive orchard.

"I know who you are, son of Stefan, and you will not find kindness here."

Amon slowly approached Taffi. The almost 100 percent humidity in the room gave his thighs a difficult time as they tried to separate and move forward. The ground pulsed as he walked, flinching with each step. Amon did, however, choose this prison for Taffi, so he didn't sigh or complain about its terrain but just kept on. As he came to the edge of the mucus mound, Amon looked down and noticed the copper emblem on Taffi's chest. The edges of the emblem, with its circular stains of dried blood, matched the color of the walls. After navigating through the sensitive spots on the floor, Amon finally chose an appropriately menacing stance and began to speak.

"Liana tells me that you are a hero, that you risked everything to come to her rescue. Can it be? Is this hero the same that has pushed disease and dementia on humans? The same that sees their pain as entertainment?"

He looked up at the dark corridor above Taffi's head and tapped his brow as if pondering some deep philosophical conundrum. "I wonder: Would she still trust you if she knew you were the one who captured that boy on *The Drunken Maiden*?"

"Noo!"

Taffi tried to speak out, but the mucus spilling over his lips only muffled his cries. If Liana knew that, he would have no one, no one at all. He began to panic. His limbs thrashed wildly within the mucus mound, trying to break free.

"And yet," said Amon, "even without your powers, she does still trust you."

Terrified, Taffi froze as Amon moved his face closer to his.

"Why? Has this copper prison given you a heart?"

Amon waved his hand again, and the binding mucus fell from Taffi's lips.

"Answer me!"

Taffi wanted to answer, he wanted to prove he was different, but he didn't know why Liana trusted him. No one had ever trusted him, not willingly at least.

"This is different," said Taffi. "I'm different; I want to help her."

"Why?"

Taffi searched his mind again, trying to come up with something profound. It had to be profound. Amon had plenty of reasons to doubt him, so this had to be big enough to trump all those feelings of hatred swirling around in Amon's head. Maybe it was simple, something as obvious as the nose on his face. He wanted to help her because...

"I don't know," he said, "because she was nice to me?"

Taffi looked at Amon as if waiting for affirmation. Amon simply shook his head. It was obvious to both of them that Taffi had no idea why Liana trusted him, nor why he wanted to help her, at least consciously.

"Because she's not human?" Taffi tried again, but Amon shook his head a second time.

"Because…"

"You want her," said Amon, "and what better conquest for the son of Stefan than the heiress of the woman he couldn't have?"

"No. I'm not doing this for me."

"Of course you are. All the Ifrit are selfish. You take humans as slaves then use them for pleasure."

"No, that's not true! I care about her!"

Amon lifted his right arm into the air and slapped Taffi across his face.

"If you truly care about her, then tell her the truth!"

Taffi's face immediately grew a dark red in color, the right side from the impact of Amon's hand and the left from embarrassment.

"I have," said Taffi.

Amon slapped him again, this time on the left side of his face.

"No! The truth about who you are, what you've done, and that when you are released from your copper prison you will become that person again!"

Taffi's face became so flushed that it was difficult to tell where the burgundy walls ended and his face began.

"No," said Taffi, "I'm different now."

Amon mercilessly slapped him again.

"You won't remember these feelings!"

"I will!"

Amon's hand flew across his face one last time.

"As the months go by, you will begin to resent her. These memories will fade, and you will hate the human in her. You will lie to her, betray her, and manipulate her thoughts. An Ifrit with a half-genie slave would be powerful indeed."

"Stop!"

And he did. Amon stopped the senseless berating and allowed Taffi a moment to think.

He would be powerful, thought Taffi. More powerful than any Ifrit, even his father. He began to think about all the things he could do to punish Stefan. He deserved punishment; punishment for naming Taffi after a horse, for calling him stupid, for calling him stubborn, for ignoring him, for ignoring his mother. It felt right. Maybe he was selfish. Maybe he was using Liana. For that, he would almost certainly be killed, or left to rot inside his burgundy tomb. His only crime was having a bad father. A bad father, thought Taffi. If Amon's daughter ran away from home, was he a bad father, too? Perhaps he should ask. At the very least, it might buy him some time.

"Send her back," he said.

"What?"

"If I brought her here for my own personal gain, then send her back."

Amon was visibly caught off guard. While sending Liana back to the human world was out of the question, it was a logical conclusion to his previous thought process.

"She belongs here, with her family," said Amon.

Feeling confident with this strategy, Taffi proceeded with the "bad father" question. "Your own daughter couldn't trust you; what makes you think that she will?"

Taffi's body was ripped from his mucus prison and sent flying across the room. His slippery throat landed securely into the firm grip of Amon's hand. With each passing second, his grip became tighter and tighter. The blood in Taffi's neck, desperate to find its way back to the heart, pushed furiously against the veins pinched closed by the grip of Amon's fist. Taffi felt his Adam's apple push up against his esophagus, and his esophagus push up against the vertebrae in his neck. There was no more room, but the chubby fingers on the back of his neck kept crushing them. His face turned purple. His eyes welled up with tears, perhaps for the last time. Of all the emotions he could have chosen for his final moments, Taffi was surprised. He wasn't afraid or mad, just surprised. Surprised that his last thoughts were of Liana's hideous purple room. He hated that color. Why didn't he tell her? Of all the things to regret, he could only think of not telling Liana that he hated the color in her room. But, even so, he somehow found himself wanting to go back there.

Amon released his grip, and Taffi fell to the floor. He gasped for breath and coughed incessantly for several minutes. And for several minutes, Amon thought about Liana, too. He still did not know why she trusted Taffi. Was fate coming back around? Was he being given a second chance? Would he get it right this time, or would he fail, like he did with his daughter?

"She should've trusted me to protect her," said Amon. "She didn't have to leave."

Taffi looked up and saw the sorrow and regret in Amon's eyes. He had never seen this look from Stefan. Taffi was an annoyance to him, a mere rite of passage that Stefan needed to complete to continue his bloodline. He didn't care about Taffi. He looked up again and saw a tear fall from Amon's green eye and glide down his puffy cheek. What must it be like to feel so wanted, so needed by your dad? Amon was not a bad father.

"Now that your daughter's heiress is here, you don't want her to leave. Maybe we're both selfish."

Amon turned away from him.

"Maybe we are."

Chapter **23**

A PLAN

There, in that burgundy room with the slimy walls and the creepy valve door, two enemies suddenly became something else. Taffi knew he had to solidify their possible coalition fast. At first glance, one might think Taffi had little to offer Amon, but as the son of Stefan, he did have a lot of inside information on the bloodline of Amon's daughter. Taffi rubbed his sore neck and throat and offered up his first contribution.

"Stefan kept your daughter's family tree from branching out," he said. "Over the years, he publically labeled them as whatever society deemed suitable for ostracism: a witch, a Nazi, a communist, a crazy person. They were left with one long, thin maternal bloodline."

Amon seemed uninterested and continued to look away. Hoping to get a bigger reaction, Taffi offered up more information.

"My father will never leave them alone. Liana's mother knew she was different, and Stefan destroyed her for it. He used a different persona, a woman named Dr. Rattner."

Still no reaction came from Amon. Taffi couldn't believe it. Amon had been searching for his daughter's lineage for centuries, and Taffi was leading him right to it. Most Marid would pay anything for this kind of information. Wasn't he listening? Was he even awake?

Taffi spoke louder, "Um, when Stefan became Dr. Rattner, he tricked Liana's mother into taking different medications...medications that broke her mind."

Still, there was nothing. Taffi cleared his throat for several seconds.

Amon finally turned to face him.

"I have heard you, Taffi. And I want you to know that I appreciate everything you are telling me. I appreciate you."

Taffi's face became flushed. He had never heard these words from anyone before. He wasn't even completely sure what they meant. Amon moved closer and put his hand on Taffi's shoulder.

"I do have one question," Amon paused, "how did he know where to find my daughter?"

Without missing a beat, Taffi replied, "He knows her true name."

Amon slowly approached Taffi until he nearly braised the nose on his face with his own jolly, bulbous snout.

"Stefan knows what happened to my daughter, and I will make

him tell me."

Admittedly cruel and cynical, Amon had preyed upon Taffi's desire for a father figure. And while Amon may have been a better father in those few moments than Stefan had been his entire life, revealing that Stefan knew the true name of Amon's daughter was a huge mistake. A mistake so big, it could lead to another war between the Marid and the Ifrit. Taffi didn't want this; he didn't want war against his people. Amon walked toward the slimy valve on the floor.

"Wait!" said Taffi. "Please don't hurt them. We can get it from him another way."

Amon stopped, for he did not want war either, and if Taffi was willing to make certain sacrifices, there was indeed another way—the binding of Stefan. He who wishes to bind a genie must have two things: a piece of the genie's possession and his true name. Stefan's greatest fear was being trapped inside an object for the pleasure of humans, and, as such, he went to great lengths to make sure this could never happen. Any who joked about it, ventured a guess, or even mistakenly called Stefan by another genie's name was imprisoned or killed. As for possessions, Stefan had none. Anything he had ever used belonged to Taffi's mother, and those who presented him with gifts were promptly beaten before the entire tribe. And so the two essential items required to bind Stefan would be nearly impossible to acquire. Still, not completely impossible.

"You wish to bind your father?" said Amon.

"Yes."

Amon turned toward Taffi again and looked at him with a devious grin.

"Then you must have something that belongs to him," said Amon, "something he possesses."

"No, I don't. I have nothing that belongs to him."

Amon started slowly pacing around the room. This time, it wasn't in a zigzag fashion but in the standard straight line, back and forth.

"Nothing but yourself, of course," said Amon.

Taffi's eyes widened as he froze in place. He was not yet of age and therefore technically belonged to Stefan. Could that be why Stefan had always sent him away? Why he constantly insulted him and made him feel like a failure? Of course, that must be the reason. And while Taffi felt grateful for finally connecting the dots of his fragmented childhood, the feeling did not vindicate his father. If anything, he now felt more anger and rage toward a man who would choose fear over his own son. And now, finally armed with a weapon that could make Stefan feel like a failure, would Taffi retaliate?

Amon could feel the wheels turning in Taffi's mind and offered up some self-serving guidance.

"If only you could think of a way to prove to Liana that you're different, that you do truly care about her, that you're not selfish, then maybe she could forgive you for your past."

Taffi knew what Amon was doing; he wasn't actually as stupid as a horse. As Taffi took a few moments to evaluate his choices, he realized that he had none. If he didn't give himself for the binding of his father, he would become an outcast. Neither Ifrit nor Marid would have him, and he would be left powerless and alone. Amon knew this, too, and as he waited for Taffi's inevitable response, he felt bad for him. After all, his only crime was having a bad father.

"You know, I don't care for her purple bedroom, either," said Amon.

Taffi looked up at him suspiciously. How did he know about Liana's bedroom? And how did he know that Taffi hated the color? Could he read his thoughts? *Yes, he could.*

"How did you know?" said Taffi.

Amon ignored his question and waddled over to the space directly underneath the large, dark corridor that ascended into darkness. He peered up into the void for several moments as if trying to detect the smallest flicker of light. The crow's feet that framed his eyes sunk deeper as his lids narrowed his vision.

"What if Stefan had missed something? What if, in all his monitoring of my daughter's bloodline, he had missed one small indiscretion of a confused and persecuted young lady searching for affection? What if there was another branch on our family tree?"

"That's impossible. I was also following the lineage. If Stefan had missed an affair, I would have caught it."

Amon turned to peer at Taffi—his eyes still squinted.

"Yes, but imagine how furious he would be to learn that he had failed in keeping the so-called abomination contained and under his control. What do you think he would do?"

"I don' know, I can't imagine..."

Taffi's eyes grew heavy. He shook his head and lost his balance. Amon could see that his line of questioning required more bandwidth than Taffi's battered mind could conjure.

"No matter! It is time for us to return to the surface."

Taffi still had questions, but, like Liana, needed to eat and rest, and was finally in a position to do so. Although for a specific agenda, he felt needed for the first time since his childhood. Amon extended his arm and accepted Taffi into his embrace.

Chapter **24**

THE MARID

Liana looked up from her thoughtful gaze into the sand and heard a long, soft cry. Far off in the distance, a high-pitched sigh rang out across the ocean. If it were visible to the naked eye, she would've seen it dash across the water, leaving the waves and seagulls in its wake and wanting more. Then, as quickly as it came, it was gone, as if it were absorbed into the brisk, powder-white sand that made up the shoreline and eventually the base of the great cliff that rose up into the sky and cut into the horizon. The sound's maker rose triumphantly out of the water, a mother humpback whale. Water fell across her back, through each crevasse and across each blemish, until it reached the ocean again. She had been circling the shoreline for hours and was in need of a deep breath. First water then a dense mist exploded out of the hole on her back. As the mist slowly floated across the water and onto the sandy beach, it became Amon, perfectly dry and fresh. Another explosion of water and mist fell to the edges of the beach and became Taffi, also perfectly dry and fresh. The mother whale had done her duty and was now free to go. She dove back into the ocean with the excitement of a schoolgirl setting out for recess and flipped her tail as if to say goodbye.

With each stride, hundreds of grains of sand flew up into the air as Liana ran toward Taffi. Before he could process his new surroundings, Taffi was trapped within her arms. He waited for a moment to reciprocate, almost as if waiting for permission. Amon nodded with that same silly smile, and Taffi placed his arms around her. It was awkward at first, like a newborn infant reaching for something he so desperately needed but didn't know what it looked like or felt like and once finally found didn't know how to hold on. His hands were cold and clammy against her smooth, warm skin. Any other girl might have winced or taken this awkwardness as a sign of rejection, but not Liana. She was patient and nurturing. She held on until his arms found themselves comfortably around her back and shoulders.

"Are you okay?" she said as she stepped back to look at him.

"I'm fine. You look great."

"Thanks," she said with a knowing smile.

"Come," said Amon, "they are waiting for us."

"Who?" said Liana.

"The rest of your family."

Before she could ask another question, a tiny, bright blue fish moved up and across Liana's face, as if swimming under water. It came nose to nose with her until they touched ever so gently and then quickly swam through the salty air and into the nearby tree line. Liana grabbed Taffi's hand and followed the path of the tiny fish.

The trees were dense. Each branch that was brushed aside only revealed two more. Liana let Taffi's hand go and forged a narrow path through the leafy fortress. She spotted a clearing up ahead and walked even faster, leaving Taffi several feet behind. Finally, the branches and leaves started to move out of the way for her. She stopped in wonderment as the jungle opened up in welcome to her. Two giant leaves beckoned her to keep going. She did, and as she stepped out of the dense jungle into the clearing, she was met with a sight more magical than the most brilliant display of fireworks. Hundreds of different-colored pairs of eyes—green and blue, yellow and brown, black and white, brown and blue—they all stared at her in disbelief.

Still wearing that silly smile, Amon appeared by her side.

"My fellow Marid. This is Liana, the heiress of my daughter."

A dolphin leapt up from behind Liana, called out across the sky, and fell back down stopping just short of the jungle floor. All of the Marid cheered out in triumph! The dolphin flipped his tail fin and swam through the crowd as if navigating its way around fish in the ocean. Liana smiled as she lost herself in the crowd of what seemed like adoring fans, embracing and welcoming her at every turn.

Taffi had finally made his way to the entrance of the clearing and peeked out cautiously. The trees had not made a path for him, only snapped back and slapped him in the face. But he didn't care; he was still flying high from the long embrace Liana had given him. And even though he was temporarily left to fend for himself, he was happy that she was happy. Besides, Amon would protect him. Amon. Where was Amon?

As the rules of traveling through short distances of time and space didn't seem to apply to Amon, he was now standing high above the clearing on the monolithic cliff. He looked down on the celebration, this time without his silly smile. Another Marid joined him by his side. With a torso barely thicker than his long and lean limbs, this Marid was built like a giant stick bug. *Perhaps he was the center of their basketball team.*

"Why did you release him?" said the stick bug Marid.

Amon didn't answer immediately. It was almost as if he was second-guessing himself.

"I have my reasons," he said.

As the general of the Marid Army, the stick bug Marid was exceedingly loyal to Amon. However, that kind of loyalty meant that he also had to protect Amon from himself.

"You think he will betray his father?" said the stick bug Marid.

"He will."

As any good general would, the Stick Bug Marid immediately sought out an alternate solution, a plan B. Of course, he knew what he would do. He was the heavy, the muscle, the heat—the one to call upon when diplomacy and subterfuge have failed. It was his job to get the proverbial "it" done.

"And if he doesn't betray him?" said the stick bug Marid.

Amon did not want a fight, but Stefan had crossed a line, and there were consequences for crossing that line. "We will go to war and settle this dispute for good."

The stick bug Marid was satisfied, almost happy. Teachers teach, surgeons operate, and generals fight. That was his purpose.

"I will get my soldiers ready."

Chapter 25

SUNSET

Deep within the dense trees and bushes of the island that played host to that giant jagged cliff, an enormous celebration was in full swing. All of the Marid, each dressed in provocative white garb, danced in and around one another. It was as if the genies, trees, sand, water, and sea life were all part of one big circulatory system. The music came straight from the island. Wind whistled through the trees, and the ground rumbled a rhythmic bass. Fish of all shapes and sizes decorated the clearing as they swam through the air. Eels were like streamers, tiny coral fish like confetti, and jellyfish were like strobe lights as they all moved in sync to the beat of the tremors from the earth below. It was a rousing house party if ever there was one.

While Liana was enjoying herself on the dance floor, Taffi remained comfortably hidden behind the tree line. Still, he didn't feel left out or abandoned. As the Ifrit never had celebrations like this, he wouldn't know what to do if he were out there. It was better that he just observed. Liana continued to dance until the same blue fish from the shore came nose to nose with her again and then dashed over to the tree line where Taffi hid. Liana's eyes lit up, and she rushed over to him.

"What are you doing?" she said. "Come and dance."

Taffi promptly hid behind a large leaf.

"No, no. I couldn't."

Liana reached into the green fortress and grabbed him by the hand.

"Come on," she said, "don't be silly."

"No! You don't understand. They don't like me."

Liana reached in with her other hand and grabbed ahold of his collar.

"That's because you're not dancing."

She gave a big tug, and out he came.

"Wait!"

Before he could say another word, Liana dragged him out into the middle of the clearing. Some of the Marid stopped dancing and looked at him suspiciously. They all knew who he was, and they all hated Stefan. Surging from all the confidence bestowed upon her from her celebrity-like welcome, Liana put her hands around Taffi's neck and began dancing. Without a choice, Taffi slowly began to mimic Liana's moves. He was awful. Like plaque in an artery, Taffi had caused this harmonious circulatory system to shut down. More of the Marid stopped dancing and peered over at Stefan's son. Was it possible that they would hate him even more now? Once again, the tiny blue fish from the shore came to his aid and bit him gently on his left hip. Taffi jerked right as Liana moved left. The tiny blue fish bit him again, this time on his right hip, and as Taffi jerked left, Liana moved right. Two eels quickly joined in the cause and curled themselves around Taffi's arms. Three more fish came, too. Before long, the sea creatures had taken control of Taffi's body, and he was dancing with Liana like a pro.

The other Marid continued to watch, and a few started to smile. It appeared as though the island had accepted Taffi, so perhaps they should, too. The Marid and the Ifrit were, after all, in a truce—a cold truce, but nonetheless, a truce. There was no fighting between them, but then there was no talking, either. Perhaps on this day and on this island, their cold truce would start to thaw a little. The other Marid started to slowly join Liana, Taffi, and the accompanying sea life in dancing. Before long, the celebration was in full swing again, and Taffi began to come up with some moves of his own. Liana tried as hard as she could to contain her laughter as Taffi jerked his limbs in what seemed like some combination of the Cabbage Patch and shoveling. He knew she was on the verge of hysterical laughter, and he loved it. While Taffi was initially trying to fit in, he quickly saw that it was his awkwardness that Liana liked, not his ability to be like the others. After a while, it became a game; Taffi would try a ridiculous new move, and then Liana would try to copy him without laughing. And in the midst of it all, if only for a few moments, they both forgot about being cursed and disappearing from Jamison, and just had fun.

As Taffi and Liana swept through the clearing like a pair of epileptic Roombas, their eyes met often, each time acknowledged by a smile, a subtle wink, or a giggle. When they finally came to the other side of the tree line, Taffi looked at her a little bit longer than usual. Behind her, through the trees, he saw a group of fast-moving clouds shoot across the sky and gently grabbed Liana's arms.

"What are you doing?" she said.

"I want to show you something."

Liana could see the excitement on his face and followed him back into the tree line. This time, the trees parted for them both and made a path back to the shore. As they reached the white, powdery sand, Taffi suddenly stopped and looked up at the horizon.

"What is it?" said Liana.

"Look," Taffi pointed up to the fast-moving clouds overhead.

Liana looked up and saw them sweep across the horizon like giant paintbrushes, leaving brilliant colors in their wake.

"What's happening?"

"It is said that the Marid paint the skies when they celebrate," said Taffi. "I have never seen a celebration this grand."

Liana looked up at the giant sunset. It seemed to cover the entire planet, comforting it in a soft blanket of lavender and violet. She could almost smell it. It was all at once provocative, overwhelming, and therapeutic. It couldn't all be just for them. How many others would notice it? A hundred? A thousand? Maybe millions across the earth? How many were just like them, cultural enemies brought together by chance. *Or was it by chance?*

Liana gently took Taffi's hand and leaned her head on his shoulder.

"It's beautiful," she said.

Taffi looked down at her. He didn't know which was more beautiful, the sunset or Liana. He wondered, for a moment, if things were different, if there could be a future for them. He thought about all the things Amon had said, that once his powers returned he would forget these feelings and begin to resent her. He couldn't imagine resenting her. But then again, he couldn't have imagined that he'd be standing here, hand in hand, with the heiress of his father's betrothed, either. Taffi pulled his hand away and turned to look at her.

"I'm sorry," he said.

Liana smiled.

"Sorry? For what?"

"Those things I did to your father, and the girl at school. I…I'm sorry."

Taffi turned away from her, but Liana persisted.

"It's okay."

"No, it's not."

There was much more to confess, but Taffi couldn't bring himself to admit it. He hoped this much would be enough, that it would vindicate him for all the unsaid crimes he had committed against humans or that he would commit. But he didn't know, and all he could do was beg.

"I'm sorry. I was wrong. I promise I'll make it up to you. I should've known my father was—"

"Stop!" said Liana.

She gently took his hand again and looked him in the eyes. "It's okay. You risked your life to bring me here. I think that makes up for it."

Taffi smiled. He was not sure that was true, but, for the moment, he would take her word for it. Liana's eyes started to close and her lips began to reach out for his. Most people who find themselves about to be kissed for the first time will say that they neither heard, tasted, nor felt anything else, that all their senses focused solely on that first kiss. Taffi, however, heard, tasted, and felt everything else. And as a rogue fruit fly took a pit stop on Taffi's left ear, he flinched and caught Liana's kiss squarely on his right cheek. Liana was surprised but still smiled politely.

Taffi began to panic. His arms went numb as his blood seemed to dance inside him. It was as if each cell in his body were screaming out, "Kiss her!"

Liana was embarrassed, too, but had seen this many times before with other fledgling couples in a semi-private corner of the high-school halls. Standard protocol suggests filling the awkward silence with a benign comment, maybe something about the weather or that really difficult algebra exam.

"Um, thank you for showing me the sunse—"

But before Liana could finish, Taffi soared in for redemption and kissed Liana gently on the lips.

Chapter 26

PUSH WHAT?

I stared at the tightly closed shutters of our modest gray colonial house, wanting to open them, wishing for someone to help us. But no one could, and no one should. For this was uncharted territory, and like so many brave explorers before us, Alexander and I had to chart this new world alone.

"Push!" said Alexander.

I stared back at him through the stinging sweat in my eyes. "Push what!?"

"The baby!" said Alexander as he placed another cold compress on my forehead.

Lying in bed with my legs apart, I reached above my pregnant belly and began to push down on it.

"No," said Alexander, "push from the inside!"

I looked at him with the disdain that only a woman in labor could conjure.

"This is not how I was born," I said.

Most colonial women, so I heard, endured labor for ten to twenty-

four hours. I, of course, thought I could do it in ten to twenty-four minutes.

"How can humans do this!?" I said. "It's so primitive, like you're an animal!"

Alexander paid no attention to the extremely bigoted comment I had just made about his people, and he got another compress. It's amazing the things pregnant women get away with.

Almost as quickly as he put the cold compress on my forehead, I called out in agony. The skin on my stomach began to stretch up and out toward the ceiling of our modest house. For the first time, I could feel the baby's thoughts. She wanted to come out; she wanted to forge her way into the world with confidence, as any pioneer would. The first of her kind, she wanted those who came after her to know that she was proud of her fate before it even began. And, like Lucy the Hominid, she would leave a legacy of mystery and wonder for centuries to come. I called out in agony again, this time even louder. Alexander could not, and would not, stifle me but feared a passerby might hear the noise and expose us. He quickly grabbed a blanket and wedged it into the crevasses of the closed shutters.

Then, there was a moment of silence. He looked back to find my eyes had gone completely black, and the baby's head was crowning.

"I can see the head!" he said.

He huddled in between my legs and grabbed my hands.

"You can do it, honey," he said. "We're almost there!"

I screamed again, this time without stopping. The sound grew deeper and deeper until it exploded into a tiger's roar. The blood vessels in my head and neck bulged several millimeters off my face and become black in color. My skin turned orange, almost as if I were transforming into a tiger. Suddenly, Alexander called out in agony and ripped his hands away from my tight grip. Blood gushed from deep cuts made across his palms. My hands, also orange and black, had grown razor-sharp claws. The faithful mattress below me, soaked in blood and sweat, was the next victim. I let out another roar and thrashed about, ripping the mattress to sheds. And then, amidst all the blood, feathers, tears, and screams, the faint cry of a baby was heard. I slowly melted back into myself and looked up at the most beautiful sight I had ever seen.

Chapter 27

MORA

Liana was awake but didn't want to be. She wanted to keep dreaming, to see the face of the ancestor that she shared so much with. What color were her eyes? Her hair? How tall was she? Liana concentrated on the dream but couldn't fall back into it. *I had grown tired from recalling that memory.* The inside of Liana's eyelids could only filter out so much sunlight before appearing bright red, a red that kept her mind alert and hungry.

"Another dream?" said Amon.

He had been standing above her for quite some time, waiting, watching for something. But what, Liana didn't know. She opened her right eye just enough to confirm her surroundings. It was that same room made of sand. The table and chair where she had so gracefully stuffed her face with the fruits of the island were gone, and in their place stood a large bed, also made of sand. Like her memory foam mattress at home, Liana had melted right into it. She pushed down on it with her hands as she propped herself up, but instead of conforming to the shape of her palm, the sand mattress seemed to push back up at her and then gently nudge her over to the edge, like a wave guiding a surfer to the shore.

"You were dreaming?" said Amon.

Liana stood up and looked at him suspiciously. "Yes, she, um, I mean your daughter, was giving birth."

Amon smiled sadly. How he wished he could have been there for that moment. To see his granddaughter's birth, not just as a grandfather, but as a witness to history and legend. It was a once-in-a-millennia moment. How wonderful and terrifying it must have been. Wonderful and terrifying, he thought. And as he thought, he realized that he missed something far greater than a legendary birth. She must have been so scared—*I was*. Everyone thinks that these legendary moments are cathartic, but in reality, they're terrifying. And he missed it. He was supposed to protect and support her in moments like these, and he didn't. He couldn't. He failed. This regret laid upon him so heavily that his face began to harden.

"Amon?" said Liana.

He broke out of his thoughtful trance and looked at her.

"Yes, giving birth, good," he said, "then you are almost ready."

"Ready for what?"

The bed behind her slowly melted back into the ground, and Amon walked over to stand in its place and face her.

"To trap Stefan," he said. "He knew my daughter's true name, so I suspect that she knew his. She was very cunning and would not reveal her name without first knowing his."

Amon shuffled over to the mouth of the sand room and walked out onto the great cliff hanging over the sea. Liana did not follow him but took his place above the spot on the floor where the bed was just moments before.

"Come," said Amon, "we must practice."

The wind slowly hit his face and body, sending him into the sky as a cloud of sand. Liana looked around for some mode of transportation. Suddenly, she was sucked into the ground like a camel in quicksand.

The grains of sand gently settled on the jungle floor next to another patch of sand and took the shape of Amon. He reached into the sand patch, felt around for a moment, and then pulled out Liana. Stunned, she gasped for air and coughed up a little sand.

"Why did you do that?!"

"What? The other genies love to travel that way."

Liana tried to brush the sand off her body and hair. "Well, I'm not like the other genies, and there's sand in my hair!"

Amon knew the sand pit was a little unpleasant, especially without warning, but he needed to toughen her up to fight Stefan. And although he did feel mildly bad about it, he maintained a hard look and continued without any visible remorse.

Liana could tell by the look on Amon's face that he didn't care. His expression was still hard, like it was back in the sand room. Where was his silly smile now? Or perhaps this was the real Amon, and the silly smile was just a salesman's trick to win her loyalty. Or maybe it wasn't a big deal at all, and she just wasn't used to being treated like a genie.

"A genie's name is more than just a name," said Amon, "it is written in the stars on the day of our birth. Only its owner can see it. It commands us, grounds us, and keeps us from becoming too powerful. I am certain my daughter knew Stefan's true name, and your dreams will soon reveal it to you."

By now, Amon had walked several paces away from Liana and was standing by a thick tree. There was something odd about it. Was it moving? Liana stepped closer to Amon until she clearly saw something, or someone, behind the tree. Without warning, a dark green hand with long black fingernails made its way around the trunk. Its skin was pockmarked and ashy.

"What is that!?" said Liana.

"That is a Ghul, the lowest form of the genie. They feed off the dead like scavengers."

Amon reached behind his white garment and pulled out a small bag made of burlap fabric and leather string with one hand and a small metal object with the other hand. He then tossed the bag over to Liana, who reluctantly caught it.

"What's this?"

"Her teeth."

Liana dropped the bag as if she were holding a severed goat's foot.

"Her true name is Mora," said Amon, as he handed Liana a small brass locket—*at least my prison was made of gold.* She could see this wasn't something disgusting and took it.

"Go ahead," said Amon.

Liana stared at him like he was asking her to use a VCR. "What?"

"Bind her to the locket."

Liana didn't want to disappoint him, but she also had no idea what to do. *Will his face turn even harder if I can't do it?* she thought.

"I don't know—"

"You have the Ghul's name and her possession, and that is all you need."

He had gotten harder, and now Liana felt even worse. Suddenly that sand pit wasn't looking so bad. Faced with the choice of standing there like an English major in Chinatown or asking another defaming question, she chose the latter.

"What do I do with them?"

Feigning annoyance, Amon answered, "Place her tooth in the

locket and call her name. The rest is up to you."

And with that, he turned and began to walk away.

"Where are you going?!" said Liana.

Just before his mouth blew away in the wind to join his counterparts, it plainly spoke, "Out to lunch."

"Wait!"

Amon was gone. The Ghul began to make her way around the tree, pressing her disgusting razor-sharp nails into its bark as she moved closer. The pockmarks on her skin had made the terrain difficult for the various small insects to navigate, as they made their way up through the back of her neck and into her leathery hair. The Ghul's skin was all ashy but for one wet spot underneath her chin where rose-colored drool oozed past her freshly chapped lips. Liana picked up the small burlap bag and looked inside. Like months-old blueberries that had grown a spotted mix of white and gray fuzzy mold, the handful of Ghul's teeth nearly caused Liana to vomit. She closed her eyes, tipped it over and shook it, hoping at least one of the teeth would find its way into the locket beneath it. Mora looked at her teeth, all but one lying on the ground, and shrieked. Liana again felt nauseous; even the Ghul's voice was somehow disgusting. For fear of losing her lunch, Liana thrust the locket out in front of her and shouted.

"Mora!"

The Ghul stopped for a moment, as if remembering an errand that she forgot to do earlier, and then lunged at Liana like a rabid sea lion. Liana spun out of the way like a seasoned matador. Again she held out the locket, tooth enclosed, and shouted.

"Mora!"

The Ghul stopped again. This time she looked sad, almost forlorn. Liana couldn't help but notice a tear beginning to form in the Ghul's right eye. The poor thing, she thought. It wasn't her fault that she was born this way. Maybe she needed a hug. Come to think of it, she was so disgusting, she'd probably never been hugged. Liana wasn't about to be the first one to do it, but still she felt badly for her. No sooner did she take one step closer than the Ghul lunged once again, this time landing heavily on top of Liana. She screamed. The locket had been knocked out of her hands. The Ghul's porous fingertips squeezed her neck as rose-colored drool oozed its way down to her cheeks. Liana gasped for breath with no success. Her eyes grew heavy and began to fade then suddenly started to glow.

"Get off!"

And with that, the Ghul flew into the air like a rag doll until crashing into a nearby tree. The Ghul tried to get up but mistakenly caught Liana's gaze. Her ashy skin became whiter and whiter until it froze into a solid block of ice. The sympathy Liana had felt only moments before had been replaced with venom and rage as she pushed the frozen Ghul to the ground, shattering her body into a thousand disgusting pieces. As Liana walked past Mora's remains, her eyes dimmed back to their normal state. The smell was unbearable, like a squashed block of moldy head cheese. Liana looked up at the cliff that hung over her like an athlete dangling from a long thin pole just before it vaulted him up and over a bar suspended high above the ground. And like Amon had done just moments ago, she blew up and away as grains of sand in the wind.

Chapter 28

ANOTHER HEIR

It was as though they were an ant colony venturing out into the forest to forage for food, each a separate body sharing a single consciousness. One by one, each grain of sand followed the next, over branches and across the jagged edges of the cliff. They split into separate lines, as if challenging each other in a race to the top. The fastest, the leader, reached its final destination only a split second before hundreds more joined. That split second was all it took for the stick bug Marid to vanish from Amon's side. As the rest of the sand came together to materialize back into Liana, Amon turned toward her with a mouth full of kale and peaches. And although she was happy to see him—mostly, like a sixteen-year-old with a new driver's license, to boast about her new mode of transportation—there was something deep down inside her that felt unsure, a tiny speck, a grain of doubt. Was there something he wasn't telling her?

"We want to command Stefan, not kill him," Amon garbled.

His silly smile quickly turned to puckered lips as they held back the juices only a combination of kale and peaches could create.

Liana was disappointed. It was clear Amon couldn't care less that she had learned to travel as he did. Instead of boasting, she retreated into an apology.

"I'm sorry. I didn't mean to kill her." Liana sat on the edge of the cliff, defeated.

"You must learn to control yourself," said Amon, as his tongue freed the last bit of kale from his front tooth.

"I know. I don't know how it happens."

Amon hobbled over to the edge of the cliff and sat next to her, his feet dangling over the edge just as hers did. "For a genie, to think of something means to do it. If we consider something, it happens. If something has not happened, we do not know of it."

Liana glared at him. Although it was just a statement of fact, the words seemed arrogant and condescending, like something a spoiled pop star might say. Trying to remember that she was not around humans anymore, she replied in kind.

"I don't get it."

"That is why you cannot do it."

Liana turned her attention toward the island, searching for answers. And there were answers, many of them. Just like the millions of species that hid under the thick canopy of trees on that island, the truth lived with her, around her, and underneath her, if only she could see it. Liana thought again about how her mother must have felt: confused, powerless, cast aside.

"If she couldn't control it, then how can I?" she said. "How am I different?"

Amon thought for several moments. He knew that she would not be ready in time. Her emotional walls were too thick. She would not leave their safety and climb over them unless the stakes were even higher than they already were. Yes, the love she felt for her father was great; it had gotten her this far, but it wasn't enough. She needed more than love. She needed rage. Love is perhaps the most powerful feeling on earth, but rage, rage can move mountains. If she would not climb over her walls, perhaps she could break through them.

Amon leaned in close to Liana's ear and whispered, "Your mother couldn't control her powers, but your father could."

"What?"

Amon rose from the edge of the cliff and began to pace in a semicircle around her. A trench formed in his path almost before his feet could plough through the top layer of sand. The cliff suddenly seemed higher, and the air felt colder. It was as if the great sand room became an extension of his conscious.

"Didn't you ever wonder how your father became such a great magician?" he said.

"With practice," Liana replied without missing a beat.

Although her environment seemed to close in around her, Liana didn't notice. Still irked by her failure to control her powers and Amon's failure to commend her sand travel, Liana remained firmly planted in an adolescent mindset.

"Aha," said Amon, "with practice."

Liana could feel the mockery on Amon's face and immediately rose to her defense. "Yes, Jamison's tricks are just illusions. I've seen how he does them."

"Have you?"

"Yes."

"It is not at all odd to you that in a family where both the mother and daughter are the descendants of magic beings the father is a professional magician?"

"What are you saying, that he cheated?"

"No."

"That my mother helped him?"

"No."

"That I helped him?"

"No."

"Then what? That my father is a descendant, too?"

Amon stopped pacing and faced Liana. "Family trees have been known to cross branches now and again."

Liana thought for a moment. A million more questions

flooded her mind.

"It doesn't make any sense," she said. "He would've said something."

Her mind finally left its temporary home in adolescence, but instead of progressing, it moved backward into a childlike state. Amon's illusion of height and temperature took hold, and Liana became cold and dizzy. She sat in the middle of the semicircle carved out on the sand floor and held her head in her hands.

"Your father is another heir of my daughter, but he does not know it," said Amon.

He placed his hand on her shoulder. A feeling of relief immediately overtook her. The thought that Jamison was a descendent of a genie, knew about it, and never told her was almost unbearable.

"And that is why he can control his powers," said Amon, "because his mind is not bound by its own expectations."

"Whose mind?" interrupted Taffi.

Both Liana and Amon looked over at him. How long had he been standing there? While Liana trusted him, even cared for him, she knew that this information could be a game changer for Stefan. It meant that there might be others out there like her, possibly dozens. So for the first time since they'd met, Liana decided to withhold something from Taffi. She stood up and put her acting hat on.

"My mind," she said.

"Your mind?" said Taffi.

"Yes, I'm still having trouble controlling my powers."

Amon was not only impressed with Liana's emotional transformation, whether real or conjured, but he was also pleasantly surprised by her loyalty. This was the first time she chose to trust him over Taffi.

"Well," said Amon, "Taffi has been using his powers his entire life, up until now, of course. Perhaps he can show you a thing or two."

Taffi smiled. "Perhaps I can."

Chapter 29

MADI

Each moved to create a path. Some were smooth, symmetrical, and lush, while others were jagged, dried out, or even broken. No matter what its condition or status, each leaf and each branch bowed to make way for Taffi and Liana, like royal subjects genuflecting to their king or queen. This time, however, Taffi was the leader. He moved with purpose and promise. And while he might have been happy with life on that island just as it was, even for eternity, the reality of his situation would not allow it. He needed Liana to control her powers, if not for herself, for him. He needed her protection in the fight that would inevitably come. He needed her protection from Stefan. Taffi looked back at her for a moment and wondered how much longer it would take her to understand.

"How did it go with Mora?" he said as they leapt over a fallen tree.

"Oh, well, I wasn't able to bind her."

Taffi tried but could not meet her eye. She was clearly embarrassed.

"Don't be discouraged," he said, "it was only your first time out."

"Right. I did manage to kill her, though."

Taffi tried to stop his eyelids from expanding, but the fear of being accidentally vanquished sprung them open like an over-caffeinated Venus flytrap. Unable to move, Taffi let Liana take the lead for a moment.

"I don't understand what I'm missing," she said. "It's not like quantum physics or something."

Now Taffi's eyes grew even bigger. Perhaps it was like quantum physics, he thought. Perhaps that was the key to helping her understand a genie's powers.

"Actually," he said as he rushed up past her, "controlling your powers is exactly like quantum physics."

The mere suggestion of this made Liana even more self-conscious.

"Great," she sighed.

"No, really, in the world of quantum physics, reality does not exist until you are looking at it."

"This isn't really helping."

"Just listen. The things you humans call particles or protons have no physical properties until they are actually observed. And there is no way of knowing what they will become once they are observed. You can only predict the likelihood of them becoming one thing or another."

"Still not helping."

Taffi could tell she was not paying the least bit of attention. This must be how teachers feel, he thought. Taffi skipped ahead and turned around to get eye contact.

"If a tree falls in the woods," he said, "but there's no one there to see it fall, does it still fall?"

"Yes?"

"No. According to quantum theory, it has only fallen once you've seen it, or once something in the future knows that you will see it."

Liana conjured up her best "oh, now I get it" face and smiled.

Taffi bought it and continued on, "Humans do not know what a particle will become once it's observed, but genies do. Not only do we know, but we can manipulate these particles through space and time as we wish, or in some cases, as our masters wish."

As they continued through the dense trees, Liana feigned her interest in the gobbledygook that was coming from Taffi's mouth. Just as she was about to ignore him completely and worry about her father, something suddenly clicked. She remembered what Amon had said, *"To think of something means to do it. If we consider something, it happens. If something has not happened, we do not know of it."* Could this mean that if Liana simply thought of something, it would happen? She stopped for a moment, and for no other reason than her current train of thought, a thousand tiny points of light seemed to dance around in the space before her. It was like what someone might see right before he passed out into an unconscious state. Just as Taffi concluded his verbal dissertation on Schrodinger's something-or-other, Liana reached out and held some of the tiny flickering lights in her hand.

"And so the cat isn't alive or dead until you open the box and look," said Taffi.

He turned toward Liana for some kind of verbal or even physical confirmation that she was still listening and saw that she was holding a small cat in her hand.

"Where did that come from?" he said.

Liana had no idea; she knew only that the lights had been in her hand, and now they were gone. Not confident enough to consider that she may have just used her powers, Liana conjured up her best lie.

"I don't know. I just saw her running across the path and picked her up. I hope she's not lost."

Completely uninterested, Taffi responded, "She must belong to one of the other genies."

Liana set the cat down and watched her scurry off into the wet bushes. The events that had taken place over the last few days were so bizarre and non sequitur that a cat mysteriously appearing in her hand from a bunch of tiny lights didn't quite make the connection in Liana that it should have. She was just grateful that the conversation was over. Feeling satisfied and even proud of the explanation he had just given Liana, Taffi had also lost his grip on reality, as Liana had clearly been ignoring him during most of his speech.

And so, Taffi took her onward, past the clearing below the great cliff, through the thick brush of the forest, and into a small ravine near the beach. Liana slid down into it and was greeted by a dead fish. The lifeless sea bass wasn't alone; several more were scattered all over the ravine.

"What happened here?" said Liana.

Taffi turned to look at her with a furrowed brow.

"The fish."

"Oh, the fish. During the tide the sea water sometimes spills over into the ravine."

How sad, thought Liana. With the rise of every tide, some unsuspecting sea creature was carried by chance into a veritable prison. She looked down into the eyes of the empty fish that lay at her feet.

Taffi could tell Liana was drifting into her own emotional prison and attempted to bring her back to task.

"Once Stefan is trapped, he must do whatever we wish, but he will only do so as a reward for freeing him."

Liana would have ignored him, but the word *wish* broke through the emotional membrane surrounding her and fell comfortably in her ear.

"I thought it was three wishes and then back in the lamp?" she said.

Taffi continued to walk forward and Liana followed.

"No," he said, "once the wishes are granted, the genie is free."

A cluster of mucus-like fluid spurted out of a dead fish as Taffi carelessly stomped across the floor of the ravine. Liana, on the other hand, had taken care not to step on any dead fish and danced around behind him like a soldier navigating a minefield.

"There is always one request that the genie is prevented from granting," said Taffi. "If you ask it, he will be freed immediately, and all your wishes will be reversed."

"How do you know what not to ask?"

Taffi stopped. "You don't."

He was successful; Liana was now back on task. She looked past him and noticed a large metal pot filled with gold. A beautiful rainbow leapt up out of it and soared across the cloudless sky.

"Look!" said Liana, as she dashed past Taffi to touch it.

"Wait! The pot is enchanted; it holds a genie."

Liana stopped just short of the base of the rainbow. She looked inside the pot and saw nothing but bright, shiny pieces of gold.

"Is it another Ghul?"

"Yes. Her name is Madi."

"Her true name?" Liana thought this was odd. "For beings with such hard-to-get names I have already learned two of them within the space of a few hours."

"Yes, Ghuls are stupid and fall for almost anything," said Taffi.

Liana reached into the pot and ran her fingers through the gold pieces like a comb through the hair of a collie.

"Madi," she whispered.

The gold pieces in her hand began to oxidize. The entire stash of gold started to sizzle and melt before her. Liana was mesmerized. The heat pushed her back on her heels until she was thrown off balance and stumbled backward. A nearby fish carcass, which Liana had just so carefully avoided, felt the weight of her foot as it pushed the insides out. Another fish cooked on the ground near the bottom of the pot until it was buried by the overflow of melted gold. Then slowly, green scaly skin, black fingernails, and all, another Ghul emerged from the pot.

"What do you want?" said the Ghul.

Her voice had the appeal of a rabid baby raccoon. Liana, still mortified by the fish guts on her foot, looked back at Taffi with confused disgust.

"Go ahead," he said, "wish for something."

Excited by the idea of wishing, Liana pulled herself out of her nausea, looked Madi straight into her quail's egg of an eye, and commanded her.

"Madi, I wish I had a diamond necklace."

Madi's face became sour just before she vomited all over the ground in front of Liana. She, in turn, then vomited in front of Taffi.

"Well, that didn't work," said Liana.

"Didn't it?" said Taffi as he reached into the puddle of Ghul vomit and pulled out a beautiful diamond necklace. As much as Liana wanted to grab the necklace, her desire for vomit-free hands was greater.

"Do all the wishes come with vomit?"

"I don't know. Try again and see."

Liana looked at Madi again. The vomiting had caused her nose to bleed. The blood traveled down until it joined the remnants of vomit on Madi's chin to create a new substance that could only be described as burgundy tartar sauce.

"I wish she was easier to look at," said Liana.

With that, Madi vomited again, this time all over herself. Liana followed suit and vomited in front of Taffi again. Before Liana could express her disgust, Madi began to smear the vomit all over her body, and with each smear, beautiful, soft, smooth, clear skin appeared. Smear by smear, Madi was wiping herself into a gorgeous young woman.

"Wow," said Taffi, "nice wish."

They both laughed. Madi climbed out of the pot and joined them in laughter. It was like she was one of them.

"You've got one more," said Madi.

Her voice, now with the pure tone of a Disney princess, seemed to beckon Liana, almost egg her on.

"Tell me," said Madi, "what do you want?"

The ravine was quiet. Liana looked into her eyes. They were the kind of eyes that foolish men fell into, pools of pure blue light. Was she sincere? Would she really give her what she wanted? It seemed like she would. Why else would she ask? Liana looked back at Taffi. He was no help. Predictably, he had fallen into Madi's trance. But then again, Liana had, too.

"I want you to remove my curse," she said.

Madi laughed like a cruel stepsister. The diamond necklace disappeared from Taffi's hand and her eyes went black.

"Sorry," said Madi, "no can do, honey."

While her voice had turned back to that of a rabid baby raccoon, she was still quite attractive, and Taffi was still no help. The Ghul raised Liana up by the neck until the only thing connecting her to the ground was a thin string of fish guts dangling from her toes. The uglier Madi got, the more present Taffi got. Sadly, he wasn't present enough in time to dodge a giant wad of spit that flew from Madi's mouth. Her mucus struck his leg and spread out onto it like cracks in a shattered windshield. The mucus continued to connect until it transformed into a giant worm with its mouth clenched tightly onto Taffi's lower leg.

"I guess that was the one wrong wish," he shouted looking over at Liana.

"Stop her!"

But he couldn't. His powers were still trapped behind the copper emblem on his chest.

"I can't breathe!" said Liana.

Taffi looked on helplessly as Madi tightened her grip around Liana's neck. Her skin was red and flushed, as if every cell in her body were crying out for air. And for a moment, only a moment, Taffi remembered how it had felt when Amon had squeezed the life out of him back in the belly of that whale. He remembered as he looked at Liana suffering the same fate, and he felt vengeance. The feeling passed as quickly as it came but lingered on in Taffi's mind. Why did he feel vengeance? Was Amon right? Was this a preview of things to come? Would his resentment for Liana build over time until he betrayed her or vindicated himself and his people? The thoughts stung him worse than the dull, bony teeth of the giant worm slithering its way up his leg. Perhaps he should surrender to the appetite of this hideous creature. That would certainly be a better fate than betraying the one who had brought him so much compassion. The long, emotional journey that had taken place over seconds in Taffi's mind brought him back to his final thoughts when Amon's hands had tightened around his neck: the color of Liana's room. The purple paint that he hated so much. Joy filled his heart. Even as the slimy worm clenched once more on his battered knee, tears of happiness tumbled out of his eyes and fell upon the creature below. This last thought, the thought of purple paint, was evidence that although his father had planted the seeds of hatred and vengeance deep within him, his mother had also planted the seeds of love. And with that realization, Taffi knew what he had to do.

"The tree won't fall until you see it," he shouted. "Do you see her in the pot?"

"I can't..."

"Do you see her in the pot?"

Liana could not speak but instead looked at him with certainty. It was the same certainty she'd had when she pushed Stefan, controlled the hermit crabs, and killed Mora. It was the same certainty that would now allow her to bind Madi back to the pot. She did see Madi in the pot. A thousand tiny points of light traveled from the space around her into the pot until they took the shape of Madi and then vanished. Liana grabbed the Ghul's wrist and broke it in two. Air flooded Liana's lungs as quickly as she fell back to the ground below. Madi didn't cry and didn't run. She didn't even scream. She knew what was to happen next, and there was no use fighting it. Liana tore a fistful of wiry hair out of Madi's flaky skull, threw it into the pot, and commanded, "Madi, you belong to me."

And with that, Madi was sucked back into the pot, and the giant worm disappeared. Liana turned to look at Taffi's leg. There was no blood, no mucous, only the sea-salt stains and frayed holes any pair of pants would fall victim to on a several-day journey through ocean, forest, and mountains. It was as if Madi's encounter had never happened. They stared at each other for a moment. Taffi looked up at Liana with hope. Hope and fear. Did she know his dark thoughts? Could she feel them deep inside him? When the first moment turned to a second, he began to think that she did. Liana's powers and her ability to use them were completely unknown. For all he knew, she could reach into his subconscious and extract every thought, every memory, even the forgotten ones. Should he say something? Would it matter? The second moment turned into a third. Beads of sweat started to form around the colic of Taffi's hair. Her eyes began to widen, and Taffi braced for impact.

"I did it!" said Liana.

"Yes," said Taffi wiping the sweat from his brow.

"I did it! I can't believe I did it! I trapped her. Did you see that?"

"Yes," was all Taffi could say.

It was like he was playing chess against himself. Every thought, whether realistic or not, was second-guessed by the next. Was she just pretending to be happy? Was she luring him into a false sense of security? Could she read his thoughts? Did she know that he knew that she could read his thoughts? Maybe she couldn't read his thoughts. Was he acting weird? Did she think he was mad at her? Was he hugging her tight enough?

Liana pulled away and looked at him knowingly. "Not bad, right?"

Taffi still didn't know what to say or how to act.

"Right?"

Taffi searched his mind for an appropriate reaction and still found nothing. Perhaps if he played the role of the wise teacher again, he could somehow play his odd behavior off as some kind of out-of-the-box lesson.

"Yes," he said, "but we still have a lot of work to do."

"Oh."

This wasn't exactly the reaction she was hoping for. He'd just spent the last half-hour talking about quantum theory, trying to get her to control her powers; one would think he would be happy, if for no other reason than pride. Did she not do it right? Was she too slow or too fast? Was he disappointed? She, too, started to spin into a death spiral of self-doubt.

"What do you mean?" she said.

Whether she was playing him or not, Taffi liked this new exchange and settled back into his facade with confidence.

"You can't hesitate for a moment. My father could kill you in an instant, or bind you…half of you anyway."

Liana stopped and stared at him for a time. Taffi's reaction to her success had become so opposite of what she'd expected that she almost wondered if he was now trying to discourage her.

"Moving hermit crabs, pushing someone across the room— those are mere parlor tricks compared to what most of us can do," said Taffi.

Now that was just insulting, thought Liana. But even so, she did not take offense. It was as if this breakthrough into her genie-self gave her a new perspective, even wisdom. There was still self-doubt, there was no question about that, but it wasn't as crippling as before. As she watched Taffi march grumpily ahead of her, she began to recognize something in him.

"We genies are more powerful than you think," he said. "When we duel, the earth loses its balance. There are earthquakes, hurricanes, volcanic eruptions…great disasters."

Taffi felt that Liana was no longer trailing him and stopped to look back.

"Are you listening to me?!"

Aha, thought Liana. That was it. That face. She recognized his sour, unrelenting expression. She had seen it in herself several times on this very trip. Taffi was hungry. Liana smiled and grabbed a nearby fallen coconut.

"I think it's time to eat," she said.

Luckily, Taffi still had enough energy in him to stop himself from launching a strenuous objection and simply smiled. As Liana plopped herself beside a nearby rock and whacked it with the coconut, Taffi remembered the last time he'd gone fishing to ease her hunger tantrums. And even though he would have preferred to recognize this in himself before Liana did, Taffi was happy. He had seen this behavior in the couples he'd watched over decades of spying. Not all of them, though, only the strong ones could recognize the needs of their partner, despite bad behavior, and try to help them. Taffi and Liana had reached that point; they knew each other, more than most. They had seen both the dark and the light in each other's eyes and still chose to stay.

"You know," said Taffi, "as long as I'm being grumpy, I should tell you that I don't really like the color of your room."

"Oh, no?" Liana said through a smirk.

"No. In fact, I hate it."

"Well, maybe I'll repaint it then," said Liana.

"No! You don't have to, I mean, you can if you want, but you don't have to do it just for me."

They both peeked at each other and smiled. Taffi sat comfortably next to her and started scooping up crickets as they loudly revealed their locations in the nearby brush.

"Here," he said, handing Liana a live one, "these will give us more energy."

Liana wrinkled her nose in disgust, "Umm, I'm not eating that. If I can feel it moving, it's not going in my mouth."

Still short-tempered, Taffi immediately felt rejected.

"Wait!" he said as he rummaged through the tattered pockets in his pants. "They're better if you roast them."

His hand emerged from his pocket with a small golden lighter in it. There was a loop-like symbol etched into its side.

"I swiped this from Stefan's cabinet back at the theater."

Chapter 30

ESHGH

It was different now. Still modest and still gray, the colonial house seemed somehow grander and more colorful, like it had been reimagined through some kind of Instagram filter. Inside, I sat slowly leaning back and forth in a wooden rocking chair as my baby dozed off to sleep. As much as I wanted to close her eyes, the baby kept them open just a sliver, first the right eye then the left. She wanted to stay awake, to keep looking at and listening to me. And although it was just me singing, the warm lullaby that fell from my lips split into two-part harmony, then three, and then four. It was as if a choir of angels were giving a private concert for royalty in that gray, modest colonial house.

The once eager and immature Alexander entered through the heavy wooden door as a weathered patriarch. His five o'clock shadow barely hid the small scars on his face, scars that, like medals on a general, marked him as cunning and wise. The birth of his daughter had transformed him from an unstoppable force to an immovable object—from an explorer to a provider. His aura was different; it comforted instead of excited. And as he entered, I indeed felt comforted and safe. I knew that he could and would protect our baby from anything, even Stefan.

"How's our little girl?" said Alexander.

"Sleeping like a baby."

He leaned in for a kiss, first for his baby girl and then for me. We knew each other, more than most. Through all our travels and tragedies, we had seen both the dark and the light in each other's eyes and still chose to stay.

"I have something for you," he said.

"What?"

He rummaged through his tattered pocket and pulled out a small golden box with a loop-like symbol etched into its side—Eshgh, the Farsi symbol of love. He had tried to learn the language of my homeland but could never quite get it. And although he would often make fun of how mismatched the sound Eshgh was for such a beautiful meaning, he would often practice writing it in calligraphy for hours on end.

I reached out my hand and took the golden box.

"It's beautiful," I said.

"Open it," said Alexander.

I took it into both hands and pushed the bottom. It opened like a cardboard box of matches, the cover like a sleeve that comfortably concealed its contents. Inside laid a beautiful locket with a brilliant painite gem embedded on the front.

"The gem is from your homeland," said Alexander. "I took it—"

"To remind me of home."

"Yes."

My eyes began to well up with tears, both from the nostalgia of my homeland and the kindness of my husband. I looked up at him once more, and we embraced.

Chapter **31**

BETRAYAL OF THE HIGHEST ORDER

Liana awoke from the hard, damp but oddly comforting jungle floor. Dusk had just begun, and Taffi was still sound asleep lying next to her. The locket on her ankle bracelet was the same as the one in her dream, less the painite gem of course. Was it a coincidence? Of course not, she thought. Dreams are supposed to have feelings and images from reality in them. Even if it was the same locket, the most valuable part of it was gone—probably buried with a bunch of colonial artifacts that will never be found. But still, maybe that was why she was so drawn to it, because it belonged to her ancestor, *to me*. Liana reached down and gently brushed her finger against the cold metal of the locket. A brilliant flash of light forced her eyes shut. The Eshgh symbol had seared itself into her mind's eye—*sometimes people need an extra push*. It left as quickly as it came, but her head ached for several moments after. She looked at Taffi, first at his eyes and then at his pocket. The lighter that had torched at least twelve crickets faster than a witch in Salem had the same Eshgh symbol as the golden box in her dream. This meant something, she was sure of it—*yes!*—if she could just reach in and grab it without him noticing or mistaking it for some kind of physical advance. Liana confirmed that his eyes were still firmly shut and then began to slip the tips of her fingers into Taffi's pocket. Like a soldier belly-crawling across an enemy beach, her fingers slowly navigated their way across the lining of Taffi's pocket. Each wrinkle was like another sand dune to climb, another chance to be caught. Without warning, Taffi jerked and turned over onto his side. It was, of course, the side the lighter was on. Liana had extracted her fingers just in time but was annoyed instead of relieved. Perhaps she could use her powers to get the lighter out. It is either in her hand, or it isn't, right? She held out her hand and looked deep down into her palm. She studied each line, each intersection, each bulge of veins until a thousand tiny lights started to appear. She was doing it!

Suddenly a cloud of fast-moving sand glided across the jungle floor just a few feet in front of her. Liana's concentration was lost, and Taffi had now moved onto his stomach. Ready to give up, Liana turned her attention to the cloud of sand as it headed straight for the top of the great cliff. Was that Amon? she thought. Maybe he knew about the golden box with the Eshgh symbol. Perhaps it was better, or at least easier, to ask him than to try another round of pocket snatch. Liana stood up and allowed herself to be whisked up and across the island as a cloud of sand hitching a ride on the wind currents.

The wind was fast, faster than usual, and Liana appeared on the top of the cliff in mere seconds. Amon was there, as she suspected, but he wasn't alone. The stick bug Marid had him so engrossed in conversation that the two of them didn't even notice Liana standing at the mouth of the sand room's entrance. There was still something about the stick bug Marid that Liana didn't trust. Maybe it was instinct, maybe it was her genie powers, or maybe it was the very real nausea she felt from having eaten five roasted crickets the night before. Whatever the reason, Liana ducked out of sight and tried to make out their conversation.

"It's true," said the stick bug Marid, "her father has been taken into custody by the police."

"They suspect he had something to do with her disappearance?" said Amon.

"Yes, a witness reported to the police that he saw Jamison chase his daughter out of his house in the middle of the night."

Liana's face went white. With each second, her breath became more and more shallow. Her heart pounded against her chest as it tried to push each ounce of oxygen to her vital organs. The tips of her fingers became cold as her body rerouted its resources for panic. Liana's back fell flat against the outside wall of the sand room, and it gently guided her to the ground.

"And the witness?" said Amon.

"A stage worker from the theater."

Liana couldn't bear it anymore. She clawed her way back up on her feet and burst into the room.

"It's him!" she said. "It's Stefan!"

The stick bug Marid impulsively coiled himself into a predatory stance and reached for Liana's throat. Centuries of military training, planning, and anticipation had forged those stick-like limbs out of the soft, docile appendages that they once were. Though his impulses were at times rash and aggressive, they had saved countless Marid from death and capture during the great Tribal Wars of the Eighteenth Dynasty. He was a fighting machine, an aggressive force of nature, and would sacrifice anything to protect Amon and the Marid of his tribe. Although his pointy fingers stopped just short of Liana's jugular vein, she could tell he wanted to go farther but couldn't. Not because he realized it was her, but because he physically couldn't. It was almost as if something else, an invisible hand, was preventing him. Was it Amon? Was it her? Was it...?

"What's going on here?" said Taffi, as he entered the room panting.

Liana swatted the stick bug Marid's hand out of her face and approached Amon.

"It's Stefan," she said. "He must've found out about my father.

Why else would he do this?"

"Do what?" said Taffi.

"They're going to send him to the mental hospital!" said Liana. "Stefan's going to break him just like he broke my mother!"

Amon raised his hand to let everyone know, in a somewhat professorial tone, that it was his turn to speak. "It appears as though Stefan has framed Liana's father for her disappearance."

Taffi's face changed but not as expected. He wasn't surprised or shocked. Instead, he looked confused or forgetful, like he was trying to remember his next line in the high-school play.

"It doesn't make any sense," said Taffi. "Why would he do this now?"

The stick bug Marid, a little embarrassed by his overreaction to Liana, offered up an explanation.

"Perhaps he is trying to draw Liana out."

"No," said Amon, "she is a threat to him. He would not want to confront her, especially now."

Amon began to pace back and forth, once again in a zigzag pattern instead of a straight line. Taffi tried to comfort Liana as her heart continued to pound against her chest. He grabbed her hand; it was still cold, her body still poised for panic. Taffi wanted to help her, but she seemed unshakable, already past the point of no return.

"Liana is right," said Amon. "Stefan must've found out that

Jamison is another—"

"What?" said Taffi.

It was too quick. Taffi should've waited for him to finish. Amon looked at him suspiciously and started again. "Stefan must have found out that Jamison is another heir."

"That's not possible," said the stick bug Marid. "We were the only ones who knew."

"Then how did he find out?" said Taffi.

But it was too eager. Taffi could see the look on all their faces. They knew. They knew it was him.

"How long had you been standing on the cliff when I told Liana about her father?" said Amon.

Liana's heart skipped a beat, and then another, and then another. She remembered that day on the cliff; it was the first and only time she'd decided to keep something from Taffi. But did he hear them? Did he know?

"Taffi," she said, "please say you didn't tell him. Please say you didn't do this?"

But he couldn't. In the middle of the night, while Liana lay sleeping with a stomach full of coconuts and crickets, Taffi had snuck back to Madi's pot full of gold and ordered her to deliver a message to Stefan: Jamison is another heir. There could be more. He must be captured. They must be stopped.

It was a betrayal of the highest order. Liana could see by the look on his face that it was true. A deep sadness crept in through the bottom of her toes and filled up her body until it spilled out onto her cheeks.

"No!" Liana cried as she collapsed to the floor.

"Seize him!" said Amon.

The stick bug Marid leapt across the room like a circus performer on stilts and apprehended Taffi in one fell swoop. Taffi didn't resist, as he knew he couldn't. He knew of the stick bug Marid and all of the Ifrit who suffered at his hands. Even with his powers, there was no way he could escape his grasp.

"I always knew you couldn't be trusted," said Amon, "My only regret is that I never told Liana that it was you who kidnapped that boy on *The Drunken Maiden*."

Liana's ears rang with the words that had just escaped from Amon's lips. Like a penny traveling through a spiraling vortex tunnel at a shopping mall, the words *it was you* rolled across every square millimeter of Liana's ear until they disappeared forever into her mind.

"The Ifrit have gone too far," said Amon. "They have broken the treaties between our tribes for the last time."

"I will assemble my best men," said the stick bug Marid.

"It is time to remind them of their place," said Amon.

As Amon continued with his rhetoric, Liana's cold fingertips grew warmer, almost hot. She thought of the feelings she had for Taffi and all that they had shared. She thought of the compassion that she had shown him when no one else would. She kept thinking, and the more she thought, the hotter her fingertips became. She thought they knew each other, like the couple in her dreams. But they weren't like them. They didn't know each other at all. Taffi was just like the rest of them, just like her ex-boyfriend back home. Liana had become angry. Those words, "it was you," had started something in her. She could feel them burning through her ears and across her forehead. Uncontrollable images began to flood her mind: a flash of light, Amon's daughter, Stefan laughing, Amon's daughter again, another brilliant flash of light. Her head ached as she closed her eyes.

Amon could see Liana was losing control, but instead he turned his attention toward Taffi. Despite Amon's ominous glare, Taffi couldn't help but watch Liana. Hundreds of hermit crabs emerged from the sand walls to watch her, too. Something was happening. Taffi could feel the heat coming from her body; they all could. And as the sunlight began to bend around the torrid vapors surrounding her body, Liana threw her hands up into the air and let out a bloodcurdling scream. Hundreds of shells exploded off the backs of the hermit crabs as they clung to the sand walls for life.

Liana's eyes flashed with a brilliant blinding light. Her fingertips curled into her palms, igniting them with a bright blue flame. Then, like great hammers of fire, Liana slammed her fists into the floor below her. Lightning flashed across the sky until it opened up and poured on the earth below. The entire island was blanketed in one destructive deluge. Everything was soaked, all but for the cloud of sand that shot across the room and down toward the island's shore.

Amon, Taffi, and the stick bug Marid wiped the water from their eyes and looked over at the ground where Liana sat. She was gone. In her place was a small, insignificant crack. Insignificant until Amon leaned over to find that it continued down the entire cliff, splitting it in two.

"Like I always say," said Amon with his silly smile, "love is the most powerful thing on earth, but rage, rage can move mountains.

Chapter 32

A PERFECT VESSEL

The sand cloud that shot from the top of the great cliff, now split in two, landed like an enormous lead anchor into the shallow end of the ocean. Liana rematerialized several feet into the water, but it did not touch her. It was as if the ocean was afraid or was showing humble respect to the powerful being that stood in its presence. She looked across the horizon and into the water; thousands of tiny lights filled every surface, every crack, every single speck that was visible to the eye and even those that weren't. It was as if all the matter in the world was hers to mold and shape. What would they say if they could see her now, those framed fools who'd peered down at her in judgment in Dr. Rattner's green office? All the patriarchal men in their three-piece suits barely held together by strained seams holding back the bulges of over-privileged midsections. And their sons, all the sons, the heirs to men's arrogance and disrespect, would they dare to betray her now, to disrespect her now? *Would they dare to assume that I needed to surrender my fidelity for a lifetime in return for a man's protection?*

Perhaps it was them who needed protection from me!

Red-hot rage continued to pour out of Liana, a rage so toxic that not even the ocean would risk touching her feet for fear of contamination. The sea life, too, swam away from her like children running to their rooms to avoid a parent's temper—that is, all but one. One fish leapt out of the water and continued toward her through the air. Liana spotted the tiny lights that made up the fish moving closer and closer to her. This would be her first victim. This fish didn't know its place, didn't know that she was far superior, or that she was better than it. How dare it, she thought. Then, just as Liana raised her hand to eviscerate the fearless fish, the tiny points of light began to disappear and she saw the fish as it was. It was an ordinary fish, a blue fish, the same blue fish that had first greeted her on the island, the same fish that had welcomed her, a stranger, into his world without hesitation. And it wasn't until that brave blue fish reached her nose to touch it that Liana realized, in that moment, she was no better than Stefan. She was no better than all the Ifrit on *The Drunken Maiden.* Her hands started to cool, and the water gradually gave way until it washed over her feet. Liana looked into the eyes of that blue fish and smiled.

"You are my only friend," she said.

The feeling of depression that her family knew too well crept back into her head and reminded her that she was also human. She was no more superior to that blue fish than genies were to humans.

Liana's rage was colder now but still there, still pushing her to go after Stefan. How would she get to him? Traveling as sand could only take her so far; the tiny grains could easily separate and lose each other on the treacherous journey across the sea. Her feelings stretched out far across the ocean floor, through the coral reefs, and under the hidden bellies of the stingrays buried in the sand, until they came upon an old wooden ship. Liana could feel its rotted mast, covered in barnacles, reaching up to touch the surface. Her thoughts swam through the upper deck, through the grand staterooms of their once-wealthy inhabitants, down to the rusted coils of the bunks shared by the untouchables on the lower deck. She could feel the fatigue from the immigrants who'd carved such ornately crafted designs on the ship's hull, and she could hear the cries of the people who had drowned admiring them. What more perfect vessel could there be to take her on her travels than this great coffin, a coffin that did not discriminate between the rich or poor, man or woman, superior or inferior? All were the same in her eyes, and all of them met the same fate.

Liana closed her eyes, tightly at first and then more relaxed. She opened them again to see the world before her covered in millions of tiny points of light. The wooden ship, with all of its history and new inhabitants, gradually rose to the surface of the ocean. This vessel would take Liana to meet her fate.

Chapter 33

THE PAWN'S REWARD

Amon's plan had worked. Rage had allowed Liana to reach her full potential. Only now could she successfully face Stefan and bind him.

"I have done what you asked of me," said Taffi, "now free me."

Amon pulled the copper emblem off his chest, and color flooded back into his skin. He had longed for this moment of relief, yet the pain in his chest was still there. Why was it still there? The curse had been removed.

"Heartbreak," said Amon softly.

"Heartbreak?" said Taffi. "You said you would free me."

"And I have. But this kind of pain no genie can remove."

Taffi searched his mind for a solution. If only he could speak to Liana, if only he could tell her how he felt, then maybe the pain in his chest would go away.

"You cannot let her see you until it is time," said Amon, "or all that you have given will be for nothing."

All that he had given, thought Taffi. What had he given?

Taffi's mind disappeared inside itself, trying to remember what he had before Liana had seen him that day in her hideous purple room. And as he thought back to those carefree days of reckless human taunting and merciless mischief, those days of always watching and never participating, always hiding, always fearing either the disappointed gaze of his father's eyes or imprisonment at the hands of some clever human, it occurred to Taffi that he didn't have anything to give. His only virtue was helping Liana find the Marid, and Stefan's curse gave him no choice in the matter. He was simply a tool, a pawn in the never-ending chess match between the Ifrit and the Marid. Perhaps he should feel lucky, even fortunate. Surely all the pawns' hearts broke for the queen, but not all of them could say they sacrificed themselves for her, that she prevailed because of his forfeiture. Maybe that is what Amon meant—that he, however insignificant, had given himself.

With a new sense of self-respect, Taffi looked across the room at the other players: the king and his knight. His knight, the stick bug Marid, peered back at Taffi, almost as if he were trying to quell the ounce of confidence that dared to bubble up from within. It was clear the stick bug Marid still did not trust him. In fact, he didn't trust anyone but Amon, and rightly so, as it has been said that the secrets and lies contained within the stick bug's mind could turn brothers against brothers, fathers against sons, Marid against Marid.

Taffi thought about this for a moment and wondered what lies he had been told.

"Is it true?" he said.

"Is what true?" said Amon.

"Is Liana's father really another heir to your daughter?"

"No."

Taffi was surprised, not by the lie itself, but by their willingness to put Jamison in harm's way, especially considering how dear he was to Liana. Or, maybe that was the lie, and Jamison really was an heir. How could he know? Would he ever know? Stick bug Marid watched as Amon sauntered his way over to the edge of the cliff, preparing himself for travel.

"Wait!" said Taffi.

Amon turned his head only far enough to expose the pursed edge of his silly smile.

"On the cliff that day," said Taffi, "you said it was no coincidence that Liana and her mother had genie blood and Jamison was a professional magician."

Amon could feel the wheels turning in Taffi's head and immediately sought to stop them. His one green eye peered past Taffi's wet eyelashes and into the back of his skull. His feelings stretched up the cranial nerve and through the meninges until they reached the soft, wet labyrinth of Taffi's mind. Amon thwarted every wrong turn, every dead end, and every fake memory implanted by the Ifrit to fend off the Marid's gaze. Then, just as he was about to reach the inclination of doubt that had taken hold of Taffi's thoughts, he was hit by a static shock. Amon felt it. He felt the connection, no, the devotion Taffi had for Liana. It warmed his body like a soft towel fresh from the dryer. Amon left Taffi's mind and looked over at stick bug with glossy eyes. Perhaps this time, he thought, he would tell the truth. Perhaps this pawn had earned it.

"Amon?" said Taffi again. "Were you telling the truth?"

"No. Jamison is not another heir. There are no others. I said what needed to be said. Just as you did."

Chapter 34

BROKEN CURSE, BROKEN BOY

The water was calm, almost motionless, like a smooth layer of fondant concealing an unknown treat. How deep was it? What was underneath? Would those that dare breach the top layer crave it, want more, want to go deeper, or would they wince and never want again? Liana watched as her mighty vessel, held together by the rot that had once torn it apart, sliced through the water like a hot knife into the top layer of a wedding cake. It was fast—faster than *The Drunken Maiden*, faster than the seagulls flying overhead. It wouldn't be long now. Soon Liana would face the genie that, fair or not, had become the reason for everything bad in her world: all the anger, sadness, and rage that had been building up in her since her mother's first breakdown. And not just the destruction of her family—the failed tests at school, the bad soccer games, the chicken pox, chipped nails, bad hair days, all of it—everything was Stefan's fault, and he would pay. The angrier Liana became, the faster the elderly vessel went. And although she would have liked the ship to move even faster, she needed the time spent to buffer. She needed her boiled emotions to calm into a simmer. She may be stronger than Stefan, but he had centuries more experience and could take advantage of Liana's angry momentum. She had to be exact, precise, and controlled.

Liana played out a dozen scenarios in her head—luring him to the theater, trapping him in her house, exposing him to the police—each clever and even symbolic, but none would give her the cathartic release she needed.

As the sun began to set, the ocean's surface began to wake, first as little ripples, then as small waves, and finally as large crests of sea foam. Debris began to muddy the surface. Old tree branches started to volley plastic bottles back and forth across the waves in a spirited game of sea pong. And then something else appeared in the water; it was larger than a tree branch, even larger than a tree. Liana squinted her eyes to get a better look and saw that it was moving. Still primed with anger, Liana ran up to the ship's control room and positioned its bow for a direct hit with the unidentified threat. The ghostly vessel darted forward like a purebred hound on a foxhunt. The floating branches and empty plastic bottles all stopped volleying and retired into the ship's wake. Liana relished in the thought of destroying some Ifrit scout sent to keep watch or a Ghul that had followed her from the island, or even Taffi. Wait, not Taffi, not now, not yet. Not until—

"Help us!" said a raspy tenor voice.

Somehow, through the crash of the waves and the whistle of the wind, a cry for help found its way to Liana's ear.

"Over here!" it said again.

Liana raised her right hand, and the rotted ship lost its scent for the target. The inertia of the water kept it moving forward but turned it to a nonthreatening forty-five-degree angle. Liana ran down to the port side of the vessel and peered out into the dark water below. Where had it gone? The mysterious moving object had disappeared. Liana closed her eyes and stretched her feelings out across the water. There were plenty of fish, even a whale about a hundred feet down, but no sign of a person. Should she reach farther, feel deeper, or should she just move on?

"Please help!" said the voice again.

It came from behind her. Liana ran across to the starboard side of the ship and spotted three figures bobbing up and down in the water—one small person, one large person, and a small, capsized lifeboat with three words written on its side. Could it be, Liana thought? She squinted her eyes and read each letter in her head: n, e, d, i, a, m. Of course it was upside-down and backward, but the word was *Maiden*. It was a lifeboat from *The Drunken Maiden*.

"Please!" said the voice. "Help us!"

Liana was neither shocked nor excited. There was no possible way a human slave could have escaped from *The Drunken Maiden*. As the Ifrit were far too proud for a task this arduous, the imposters were almost certainly a couple of Ghuls. Did they think she was stupid? Were they even trying? Rather than revel in a sense pride and superiority to the enemy's pathetic attempt at subterfuge, Liana welcomed self-doubt into her mind. She should've trusted her instincts; she should have mowed down the masquerading Ghuls when she'd had the chance. Perhaps she wasn't ready to face Stefan. Perhaps this was all futile.

"Please, miss," said a high-pitched thin voice. "Help us!"

Liana froze. She recognized that voice. The tone, the pitch, the agony that crept in to every syllable, every breath; it was the little boy that Taffi had taken, the one that she'd tried to save on the Drunken Maiden. Could the Ghuls be this cruel, to prey upon her memories of failure and betrayal? Liana backed her way through the once-grand entrance of the ship's dining hall just behind her. She sifted through the shattered plates and glasses scattered across the floor until she came upon a sterling silver sugar bowl with its lid still resting in the custom lip it was meant for. How remarkable, she thought, that after so much destruction and turmoil this lid and its bowl were still together. There was no attachment, nothing keeping them from separating, yet there they were, together, unfettered by the rotted watery hell that had surrounded them for decades. Liana held the bowl in her hand and thought, again, of Taffi.

"Please, come back!" said the raspy tenor voice.

Liana hid the small bowl among the loose fabric of her garment and ran back to the starboard side of the ship. The same whale that Liana had felt a hundred feet down was now swimming just a few feet below the stranded boy and his older companion. Through his layers of protective blubber, he had felt her too, and had come to help. Liana nodded her head, and with a flick of his giant tail fin, the whale sent the boy and old man up out of the water and onto the deck of the ship.

This would be her test, thought Liana. She would remain exact, precise, and controlled; and before the sun could peek over the horizon to greet a new day, Liana would have learned the Ghuls' true names and trapped them within the perfect union of her sugar bowl and its faithful lid.

"Are you hurt?" said Liana as she ran toward them.

Her feigned concern was flawless. Liana took the little boy into her arms and coddled him like he was her own.

"It's okay," she continued. "You're safe now."

The little boy squeezed her so tightly she wondered if he would ever let go. The older man slowly propped himself up on his bloodied elbows. The Ghuls had left no detail unchecked, as Liana could see bruises on their wrists and ankles where iguana tails would have restrained human slaves.

"I knew it," said the older man, "I knew you would come back for us!"

The Ghuls' strategy was clear: to prey upon Liana's compassion for her fellow humans, and thus, gain her trust, but Liana remained exact, precise, and controlled. She followed suit in this game of pretend camaraderie and looked down at the little boy with a gentle smile.

"Do you remember me?" she said.

He shook his head.

"This is her!" said the old man, "the angel that tried to save us. Don't you remember? She was bitten trying to free you."

The little boy looked down at the bite marks on her hand. Liana waited for an acknowledgement, some recognition, but nothing came. It was as if the little Ghul had forgotten his line in their little play of deceit. Not knowing what to do, he simply clung tighter to Liana's neck and said nothing.

"He is tired," offered the disguised old Ghul. "We have been floating for days."

Liana studied the disguised old Ghul's eyes; the left was bloodshot, and the right was swollen shut from what looked like an iguana bite.

"I see you were bitten, too," said Liana.

"Yes."

Liana felt the disguised young Ghul shiver in her arms and thought for a moment about the real little boy and the other humans, still suffering on *The Drunken Maiden*. Their bruises and cuts were real, and their lives were all but lost. The moment turned into two and then a third. Suddenly, Liana no longer cared about being exact or controlled but precise, yes, she would be precise. Her rage was building up again, and the hot fire inside of her could no longer be sated by the use of her silver sugar bowl, no matter how noble or faithful it had proven to be.

"It must've been so terrible," she began, "to be a slave, never knowing when you would be called upon, never knowing what wish you would be asked to grant next. Not having a choice, no matter how vile and disgusting those wishes were. I can't imagine the resentment, the anger, the rage you must've felt being the lackey to some over-privileged bully, whose only accomplishment ever was being born an Ifrit. Yes, it must be terrible to be slave, like a binded Ghul."

"What?" said the disguised old Ghul.

"You must've forgotten, I'm cursed; only a genie could have seen me that day on *The Drunken Maiden*, and only a genie could see me now."

The disguised old Ghul scrambled to his feet.

"No, it's not true, I'm human!"

But it was too late; Liana had already made her move. The floorboards beneath the disguised old Ghul had split and pulled him through their jagged edges until the splintered wood pushed into the flaccid skin of his neck. Drops of dark red blood trickled from his jugular and mixed with the rot of the old floor. Liana grabbed the disguised young Ghul by his throat and dangled him out over the ocean.

"How dare you play on my feelings!"

Her nails dug into the curvature around the disguised young Ghul's Adam's apple.

"Did Taffi send you?!"

The disguised young Ghul tried to speak but could only gasp for air.

"Does Stefan know I'm coming?!" Who sent you!?"

The disguised older Ghul looked on as the scene unfolded before him and smiled. The closer the disguised young Ghul got to death, the wider his smile became. It was as if his amusement was in direct opposition to the number of breaths the disguised young Ghul could take, and before long, his smile exploded into a riotous cackle.

"You know," said the disguised old Ghul, "you shouldn't be so hard on Taffi. I mean, if you, a great and powerful Marid, can be fooled into torturing an innocent human, then what hope does Taffi have?"

Liana snapped her neck toward the disguised old Ghul.

"No! That's not possible; I'm cursed."

"Are you?" said the disguised old Ghul.

The mere possibility that this was true was enough to spare the young person, Ghul or not, and Liana dropped him on the deck like a cold fish. He lay there motionless, not yet dead, but not conscious. Frozen with the guilt of what might have happened, Liana stretched out her feelings until they reached his pale skin. She could feel each cell, crying out for air, each artery, shuttling the oxygen back and forth as quickly as it could. And although his skin began to regain some of its color, the rest of his body had surrendered and fallen into a deep sleep.

Could it be true? thought Liana. Had the curse been lifted? Was this little boy who lay struggling to survive before her real? What had she done?

"Yes," said the disguised old Ghul, "you are no better than the rest of us."

Liana rose to her feet and struck the disguised old Ghul across his face. Only hours before, she had convinced herself that she wasn't like the Ifrit, that she knew enough to stop herself from succumbing to impulse and selfishness. Perhaps she was wrong again. Perhaps she didn't know enough, and perhaps there was more to

Taffi than just good or evil, black or white. Taffi...

"If the curse is lifted, then Taffi is—"

"Free," said the disguised old Ghul, "and after tonight, I will be free, too."

He rose up out of his splintered prison to nearly double his old size and began brushing the human skin off his body like chalk off a blackboard. His fingernails broke through his fingers and continued outward until they reached his bony knees. Liana had never seen a male Ghul before, and to say this one was intimidating was an understatement. But she didn't back down; she didn't even blink. She had failed this young boy twice before, and she would not fail him again. The old Ghul roared through his dark yellow fangs and lunged forward. The blood vessels in Liana's head and neck bulged several millimeters off her face and became black in color. Her skin turned orange, and her teeth grew as sharp as razor blades. In a split second, the large old Ghul was met at the end of his lunge by a much larger, ape-like tiger. The sheer force of her roar severed the sound waves in its path until it knocked the Ghul back on his feet. In one swipe of her clawed hand, Liana shredded through his belly and sent him overboard. In her new form of terror, Liana looked around for another foe, another pawn to pick off, but only found the little boy, still unconscious from her reckless actions. She slowly melted back into herself, sat next to the boy, and gently stroked his salty wet hair.

Chapter **35**

SHOWTIME

The grandeur was gone. The magic, the mystery was all gone, replaced by the promise of cultural enrichment in the form of a technically flawless dance troupe from the Far East. Jamison's show, like his daughter, had been removed from the now, the present, the tangible. The stage no longer buzzed with vocal warm-ups or galloping horseshoes; it was no longer adorned by ancient Middle Eastern replicas or shrouded in sand and fog. The dressing rooms, though, were still filled with talented young men and women who had visions of a bright future, visions that should be given a chance to be realized, visions that didn't deserve to be snuffed out as collateral damage in a centuries-old dispute between two ancient tribes of djinn. But the talented young men and women were taking too long. Surely the costume designer could have excluded a lace or two from the form-fitting bodices that accented the contours of the talent. Time was running out, and the innocent dancers needed to be removed.

As a six-foot-long lace finally found its way through the last hole on a stretched purple top, the entire theater went black.

"Hey," shouted a female dancer, "turn the lights back on!"

"We can't see!" said *another*.

The dancers fumbled about the room until the door behind them slowly opened and pulled one of them out screaming. A flicker of lights abruptly halted the vocal chaos that followed. Each of the dancers stood frozen and silently watched as a tube of burgundy lipstick floated in front of them and wrote the words *get out* on the nearest mirror.

Liana knew this was cliché and tacky, but she couldn't help herself. There was a part of her that enjoyed watching the dancers scream and fly out of the dressing room like a group of poorly directed extras in a low-production horror movie. She had almost wished that Taffi could have been there to share in the mischief. Mischief, she thought. Like the kind Taffi used to subject her father to.

The lights went off again.

"What's going on out here?" said a male dancer. "Who's turning off the lights?"

He was joined by several other male dancers, some still in their costumes and others in their underwear.

"It's a ghost!" said a frantic female dancer.

Whether out of real fear or just good sportsmanship, the male dancers joined the women and panicked. At this point, Liana couldn't quite make out the men from the women. They were all just shapes bouncing around the stage in the warm red glow of the exit sign against the brick wall of the theater—all but one tall, ominous figure that moved slowly through the chaos, as if feeding from it: Stefan.

An ear-tingling crash silenced the room and brought the lights back up. The last two dancers to exit shouted a few choice words and dashed out of the theater.

"Enjoying yourself?" said Stefan with a sinister grin.

The stage was covered in hazardous shards of glass and crystal from the chandelier that had fallen as Liana had recognized her enemy in the dark. The sparkling stage floor was beautiful and familiar, like the thousands of tiny lights Liana would see just before she used her powers. It reminded her of her strength and heritage. She stood tall and smiled back.

"Let my father go, Stefan."

Stefan walked toward her slowly.

"But why? His absence has made you stronger. All these years of clinging to him, waiting for his permission, hoping for his approval, but most of all hiding under his protection they weakened you. He weakened you."

Liana knew what he was trying to do, and although there was

some truth in Stefan's words, she would remain exact, controlled, and precise. She saw past him to the chards of glass and broken bits of crystal on the stage floor and focused on their hundreds of tiny lights.

"I'm warning you," she said. "Leave my family alone!"

The crystal and glass began to rise up behind Stefan, "You are so much like her."

"Let my father go!"

The floating chards of glass and crystal shot into Stefan's back like a hundred darts.

No stranger to pain, Stefan barely flinched before the ground started to rumble beneath him. The shards of glass and crystal wedged into his back grew into the plates of a stegosaurus, and the rest of him followed. Liana ran to the opposite side of the stage as the now-dinosaur, Stefan, roared into the acoustic pockets of the theater's ceiling. Hoping for a better position, Liana leapt under his flailing tail but was struck viciously in the back as she neared her landing. Her head bounced off the wooden floor as she skidded across the remaining pieces of broken glass. Blood trickled from her forehead as she tried to move her legs.

She couldn't get up. She wouldn't get up. She had tried to remain exact, controlled, and precise, but she just wasn't good enough. No amount of control could make her a better genie, a total genie. She tried to find the rage that had once set her free, but it was buried somewhere beneath a mountain of doubt. She was all at once too human and too much like Taffi, mischievous and impulsive. There was no high ground to climb upon, for she was just as flawed as Stefan. Stefan rose his enormous tail once more over Liana's head and, with a great roar, forced it down upon the heiress of his only weakness, his only failure, *me*.

Chapter 36

LUCK: THE TRUE NAME OF EVIL

The charming door of our modest gray colonial house opened once more, this time by our newborn baby and me.

"Hi, honey. I'm home."

"Hello, my love," answered Stefan.

My one green eye scanned the room for any sign of Alexander but found no one.

"Where is my husband?"

Stefan delighted in the waves of anxiety that poured out of my body and settled comfortably at his feet. It remained there, energizing his hate and vengeance, like a battery finding new life from a source of electricity.

"He ran away," said Stefan. "I suspect he couldn't handle the pressures of fatherhood."

I could see him feeding off my worry and, like flipping a switch, turned my feelings into a calm confidence. I was far more powerful than Stefan and, if pushed too far, could easily take him down. And, in fact, that was exactly what I did.

In the few moments it took me to set my sleeping baby in a nearby bassinet, I had focused the thousands of tiny lights that made up my own body and begun to transform.

"I told you to leave my family alone."

As the last syllable of the command leapt from my lips, large teeth, as sharp as razor blades, stretched both upward and downward to send them on their way. I flew through the air as a large, ape-like tiger, with black veins bulging out of orange skin. Within seconds, Stefan was rendered helpless on the floor, a mere doormat for my sweat and drool. Pinned under the two-ton weight of my new form, Stefan summoned his own beast, and before any referee could declare a victory, his body grew into an equally large, ape-like black bear. Claws from each of us were almost immediately soaked in blood and fur. The bear was formidable at first but quickly became outdone by my speed and agility. He was not the only one to suffer my wrath and brutality; each piece of furniture in that modest gray colonial house was shredded, one by one, as collateral damage in a proxy war of tribes. The final piece, a handmade dresser, home to the golden box with the symbol, was shattered back into simple lumber by the weight of the lifeless bear. My baby, however, remained untouched and uninterrupted as she lay sleeping in her bassinet.

In a final show of dominance, I bit down on the lifeless bear's neck and dragged him across the room. Satisfied by my performance, I slowly melted back into myself and peered down on Stefan.

"You have abused my name for the last time," I said. "Now it is your turn."

Stefan slowly melted back into himself, or what was left of him. His eyes were swollen shut, legs broken, and midsection exposed to any splinters, filth, or bacteria that wanted to probe his internal organs. Each malady took longer than usual to heal itself, as Stefan's will was all but snuffed out. But, as his left eye opened just a sliver, he spotted the golden box with the Eshgh symbol on it only inches from his mangled body.

"Where is my husband?" I said.

"Dead."

"Xethalis!"

Stefan's consciousness slowed to a crawl. His name, his true name, captured his mind like a carnivorous plant ensnares an unsuspecting fly. The light of the room seemed to collapse around him, showing only my face, only my eyes. What little will he had was now gone, in the hands of his unintended adversary. My hands, my gentle hands, so polished, so warm, so compassionate on their own, what dreams Xethalis had of my hands welcoming him in, if not for eternity, for just one moment. There was a time when he would have gladly done whatever I wanted, true name or not.

"Xethalis," I said again softly, "where is my husband?"

"The Drunken Maiden," he answered almost immediately.

He had no choice. No power on earth, nor any star in the sky, could break the hold of a genie's true name.

As I turned away from him, Stefan's consciousness returned. Like waking from a dream, all was forgotten—all but that feeling, that yearning for me. His desire, once dormant within him, had been reignited by my grasp, my hold over him, if only for a minute. He knew what he had to do, and he grabbed the golden box with the Eshgh symbol that lay before him, opened it, and took out the locket.

"The Drunken Maiden," I said. "For this, I will sink that boat and all of your people on it."

My words were certain and severe. Stefan knew I would hold true to them and, as such, had another reason to commit the horrible crime he was about to carry out. For so long, he had feared binding, feared imprisonment, so much so that he wouldn't even impose it upon his enemies. But now, there was no choice, the lives of his people were at stake, and if anyone ever discovered his crime, that is what they would be told; not that he had to have me so that no one else could, not that he, a powerful Ifrit leader, was rejected by a woman; not that every molecule of oxygen carried tirelessly, desperately to his heart was only ever for me. No one would ever know the truth.

I continued to walk toward my sleeping baby.

"Did you like the gift?" said Stefan.

I stopped just inches short of the bassinet and turned back to him.

"What?"

Stefan spat blood from his mouth before he spoke.

"The gift? From your husband," he said. "It's funny the things these humans will buy from you."

"No!" I looked down at the locket in his hand. It was mine, my possession—my prison.

"He said it was just what he was looking for," said Stefan.

There are some things that no amount of training, practice, wisdom, or power can prepare you for. When they happen, luck is either on your side, or it isn't—luck, that fickle, friendless giver of life or death, success or failure, love or loneliness. And on this day, at that moment, luck was not on my side; for if I had spoken just a second, even a fraction of a second before Stefan, the course of things to come would have been completely different. There would be no pain for my husband and our daughter, no regret for my father, no sorrow and no persecution of my family for centuries to come. But luck is loyal to no one; and even the most despicable, vile, and evil creatures can wield it, just as Stefan did when he spoke my true name a mere second before I could cast his miserable soul back to the very desert where I first whispered it into his crooked ear.

"Accalia!"

Chapter 37

DR. RATTNER'S FINAL SESSION

"Xethalis," whispered Liana.

She awoke with pain weighing heavily upon her head and back. The horny-tailed assailant seemed to get smaller and smaller as she lay there trying to focus. Liana couldn't decide whether he was walking away or shrinking, and before she could reach her own conclusion, Stefan melted back into himself. He looked out onto the empty seats of the audience and ran his fingers through his sweat-glossed hair. Liana knew what he would do next. It was something she'd tried to put out of her mind since she had pushed Stefan across his room and into that brick wall. *Liana looked just like me.* She had heard it over and over again from Stefan, Amon, and other Marid. And since Stefan could not court her in today's world, he would almost certainly try to take her against her will. She was his second chance at a love that he now only wanted to prove a point, to win.

Despite Liana losing round one of the battle, she was still exact, controlled, and precise. She reached into her pocket, grabbed a handful of pennies, and stuffed them into her mouth like a child sneaking candy from her parents. Liana closed her eyes just before Stefan turned toward her, brandishing a sinister grin. His footsteps echoed in her mind, getting louder with each passing moment. Soon he would claim his position of dominance over her, and she would be ready.

The footsteps had stopped. There was no sound, nothing but throbbing pain pulsing through Liana's head and back. The pennies in her mouth began to taste like blood. Was it blood?

"You look just like her," said Stefan.

He looked upon her longingly, as if he had waited for this moment for an eternity. His eyes grew softer, his posture collapsed, and he leaned in to kiss Liana's lips.

Liana felt neither the touch of his lips nor the weight of his body as he leaned in on top of her. She felt only disgust, sorrow, anger, and finally rage. The rage of a thousand young women taken against their will, forced to share a man that they could never love and would never choose. She felt the stolen privilege of all the men who had ever uttered the words: "like a girl," "just a woman," "she doesn't understand," "they're not strong enough," "they're too irrational," and finally, perhaps the worst utterance, "she belongs to me." The rage inside her grew. The ground began to vibrate. Each acoustic pocket of the theater began to hum. And where Stefan thought he would find the gentle, warm touch of a lifelong fantasy, he found only pain. A pain that seared his lips and burnt his tongue.

He immediately pulled away and spewed out a mouthful of pennies and blood. Liana rose with the strength of not a hundred men but a thousand women. There was no more pain in her head or back, only hot, pointed rage.

"You trapped her!" she said.

With a wave of her hand, Stefan flew across the entire orchestra section and broke a balcony support beam.

"You couldn't have her for yourself, so you kept her from everyone!"

Liana waved her hand a second time, and Stefan flew like a damp washcloth into another support beam of the theater. The balcony was weak but still intact. Without patience to spare, Liana waved her hand once more, and the balcony of the theater came crashing down on him.

"Now it's your turn," said Liana.

She knelt down and grabbed one of the blood-soaked pennies from the stage floor. Liana leapt over to the rubble, pulled Stefan out with one hand, and grabbed the silver sugar bowl from her garment with the other. She carefully placed Stefan's blood from the penny in the bowl and looked him in the eye.

"Xethalis! You belong to me!"

There was nothing—no flash of light, no cloud, no

whirlwind—nothing but the sound of Stefan's sputtering laughter. She tried it again.

"You belong to me!"

Still nothing. Liana's rage turned to doubt, and the doubt became fear.

"You don't believe it, do you?" said Stefan.

"Yes, I do."

Did she? What was going on? She had all the ingredients: his true name, the blood, the rage, what else was she missing?

"You don't believe it because it's not real," said Stefan.

Liana looked down and saw Dr. Rattner sitting comfortably in Row H, where Stefan had been just moments before, crushed by the weight of the falling balcony.

"No," said Liana, "this is a trick."

"Look around," said Dr. Rattner.

She did; the balcony and chandelier were restored, the stage was filled with replicas of Middle Eastern relics and genie-inspired sets; even she was wearing different clothes—dowdy jeans and a sweatshirt.

"People often get worse on medication before they get better," said Dr. Rattner.

"Stop it!" said Liana.

Thoughts rushed in and out of her head like travelers through

Grand Central Station. Could it be true? How did she get there? Where had she been for the last week?

"Think about it, Liana," said Dr. Rattner, as she rose out of her seat. "All of this started the night you took your medicine. The genie theme comes from your father's show. Taffy, the horse, hurt your father just like the Taffi in your head keeps hurting him. Your mind is just playing tricks on you."

Liana looked down at the sugar bowl in her hand. It wasn't silver or grand, just cheap and ceramic, like the one in her father's kitchen. Still, she needed to remain exact, controlled, and precise.

"I don't believe you," she said.

Dr. Rattner moved cautiously toward Liana.

"Your mother didn't believe me, either. You have to trust me, Liana."

She needed an anchor, something to keep her from drifting in and out of reality. Dr. Rattner offered up her hand for Liana to cling to.

"No," Liana said as she pushed the hand.

Dr. Rattner remained calm and, like a wingman returning to formation, placed her hand back at her side.

"I can't help you if you don't trust me," she said.

Liana's mind fell into a tailspin. She tried to find those three words, the mantra that kept her grounded, but she had somehow forgotten it. She looked around the theater for something, anything odd or incongruous that she could focus on, but everything was as it should be—no shards of glass, no collapsed beams, not even a splinter of broken wood. It was all perfect. Her father's show was intact and in its rightful place. Her father…

"Where is my father?!"

"In his dressing room," Dr. Rattner answered without missing a beat.

As Liana ran toward the back of the stage, she remembered Jamison's opening night: the performers vocalizing and warming up, and Taffy, the majestic white horse that had welcomed her to the stage right before he dropped an atrocity on it. She came upon her father's dressing room door and opened it just enough to peek inside. There it was, that decades-old poster of Jamison as a little four-year-old illusionist prodigy. She pushed the door farther, exposing all the posters, one by one, until her mind was as obtuse as the angle of the door. She didn't get it. How could this be? How could she have missed this all, just minutes before? And then, through the cognitive noise of her mind came the anchor she so desperately needed.

"Liana," said Jamison.

She turned her head toward that old cabinet with the multicolored drawers, some without handles, and saw him.

"Dad!" she said as she ran and threw her arms around him.

He grabbed her tightly with his right arm but kept his left firmly on the mismatched dresser like a kickstand on a broken down old bicycle.

"Liana," he said smiling, "is everything okay?"

She looked at him with tears in her eyes. His face and hair were damp from sweat, no doubt from a rousing performance given only an hour before.

"It is now. Are you okay?"

Jamison wiped the sweat from his brow.

"Yes, I'm fine."

But that left arm was still planted on the dresser next to him. He tried to hide his feelings, to hide the numbness he felt in his arms and legs, but he was just so happy to see her—no, not happy, euphoric.

"You see, Liana," said Dr. Rattner from behind them, "it was all an illusion, like your father's magic."

Dr. Rattner entered the room and raised the crease in her lips to show her approval of Liana's behavior but was stopped by a sharp pain in her chest. Suddenly, she, too, needed to plant an arm against some sturdy piece of furniture.

"Are you okay, Dr. Rattner?" said Jamison.

She wasn't, but she couldn't interrupt this breakthrough moment with a little discomfort. Surely it would pass in a moment.

"Yes, I'm fine."

As she began to cough and double over in pain, Jamison lifted his left arm and fell to the ground.

"Dad!" said Liana.

But he had directed all his attention to Dr. Rattner, who had buckled like a straw under too much pressure from a toddler's eagerness to get at her chocolate milk.

"I know how it feels," started Jamison, "to have something burning in the middle of your chest."

Now Dr. Rattner had turned her attention to Jamison. Her eyes peered into his skull as if scolding him for bad behavior.

"I have no idea what you're talking about," she said.

But the pain got worse, and she started sweating; and as Liana watched Dr. Rattner crumble to the floor, the anchor that grounded her started to lose its grip.

"Dad, what's going on?" said Liana.

Again, Jamison ignored her and volleyed back at Dr. Rattner.

"You're right," he said. "You have no idea."

Without warning, the door slammed shut behind them. The posters and scattered furniture began to melt into the floor like cheap candles from a dollar store. Before long, Jamison and Dr. Rattner began to melt, too. Liana looked around her and felt horror—not fear or confusion—just pure horror. Without enough breath to scream, she simply froze where she stood, not sure whether she would start melting herself or start drowning in a sea of red-hot wax. Then, out of the mounds of supple wax that were once Jamison and Dr. Rattner rose Taffi and Stefan.

"Taffi!" said Liana.

She didn't know whether to hit him or hug him, so she did both. Without wishing or wanting or thinking it through, Taffi became her anchor. Things were clear again—she remembered those words: exact, controlled, and precise, and even said them out loud.

"You fool!" said Stefan, still buckled over in pain, "all you had to do was be her father!"

As he spoke, Stefan reached over to grab the doorknob behind him and was burned by its touch. He looked at the room around him and found what the wax façade was hiding: sheets and sheets of copper. Stefan looked at his son with disappointment. It was not great disappointment, for he never expected much from Taffi to begin with. He was always just a burden, a liability, a mistake; and now he would pay for that mistake.

"How could you do this to me?!" said Stefan. "To us?!"

Although still in agonizing pain, Taffi rose to his feet and stood over him defiantly.

"There was never an 'us'," he said, "plus, I can't take all the credit. Amon never did like you."

Stefan's hatred became his fuel, and he rose to meet Taffi squarely in the face.

"Then this is an act of war," he said calmly, "and when I return, you will be its first casualty."

Taffi wanted to cry. He wanted to scream and shout and strangle the genie that stood before him, but instead, he pulled a Middle Eastern lamp from the wax at his feet and tossed it over to Liana. Stefan watched as the lamp flew through the air, and before it fell into the hands of his mortal enemy, he grabbed the doorknob once more.

"Do it now," he said.

"What?" said Liana.

Stefan's hands burned against the cold copper of the knob, but he wouldn't let go—he couldn't let go—he would push into the pain until that door opened.

"You must do it now!" said Taffi.

Liana knew what he meant; she knew that his life depended on her, and she knew that she would fail.

"I can't," she said. "I don't have his possession."

"Yes, you do," said Taffi.

Liana looked around, half pretending, half searching, and found nothing.

"What?!"

"Me. I am his son. I belong to him."

He lunged for his father, wrapped his arms around him and started pulling him back toward Liana.

"I can't! There must be another way!"

Taffi and his father wrestled on the floor like two sloths struggling to remain conscious.

"I will kill her for this!" said Stefan.

Keeping true to his word, Stefan changed course and lunged for Liana. Once again her savior, Taffi clung to Stefan's legs and stopped him for a moment. Why wasn't she acting? thought Taffi. What could be holding her back? This was the moment. Without this, their entire journey would be for nothing. The night she helped him in the park, the trip on *The Drunken Maiden*, the sushi they shared on that small lifeboat, the dancing on the island, the sunset, the roasted crickets, and that hideous purple room; it would all be for nothing. Or would it? Taffi looked up and caught Liana's gaze. She had read his thoughts and felt his feelings. She couldn't let him go.

"I betrayed you, Liana!" said Taffi. "I'll do it again!"

Stefan shifted all his weight onto Taffi's neck and crawled toward her.

"And I will rip that green eye from your head!" said Stefan.

Taffi's fingers started to cramp, and Stefan began to slip away from him.

"I'm losing him. Do it now!"

"I need more time," said Liana through her tears.

Stefan lunged back, using Taffi's weight against him, and broke free of his grasp. However futile it might have been, Stefan threw himself at Liana, hoping he could somehow stop her, somehow win the day, somehow turn back time—and then it happened. His consciousness slowed to a crawl as that word rang through the now empty space inside his head.

"Xethalis," said Liana again.

The light of the room collapsed around him, showing only her face, only her eyes. Taffi, with sweat pouring from his nose and chin, used his last ounce of strength to grab Stefan's foot.

"You belong to me," finished Liana.

Blinding light exploded from the Middle Eastern lamp as it leapt out of her limp hand and onto the floor in front of her. Like rays of sunshine came to life, the bright beams wrapped themselves around Stefan and Taffi, engulfing their bodies in a cocoon of heat.

"Don't wish for me," said Taffi, "that will be the one thing he will not grant and will set him free."

She wanted more time. She wanted to try again, to make it work, to be happy, or at least content; but he was leaving, and he could never come back. She fell to her knees in defeat. She didn't know the cost of winning—no one does—not until your hand finally makes it to the top of the mountain that you desperately covet, so painfully need, and you find yourself empty. Fantasy is just that, a place yearned for that can never be reached. The carrot must always be there, dangling in front of the face, pushing onward, giving reason to go. And as smoke began to billow up from the lamp, Liana wondered, was Taffi her carrot? Was she less of a woman because of it, because she needed him like she'd once needed her father? She looked into Taffi's eyes one last time before the dark gray smoke stole what was left of his body.

"She's waiting for you," he said.

The smoke whipped around the room until it settled into a large funnel. Ferocious yet contained, the great tornado pulled its victims into the lamp until, all at once, the room was silent.

Chapter *38*

AS YOU WISH

It was just as she'd left it, that hideous purple room. Her bed was still unmade from the night she and Taffi were cursed. The dark frames from the pictures on the wall were now a lighter version of themselves, blanketed in a thin layer of light gray dust. Liana sat on her unmade bed and looked at them: a picture of her with her mother, another with just her and Jamison, and a third with her best friend Rachel. An ornate ceramic plate, meant to showcase their Armenian heritage, sat in the middle of the pictures separating each parent, a reminder of just how distant they were. A single strand of web traveled down from the plate onto a bouquet of inverted, dried-out flowers, a gift from Jamison for her first school play. Was the spider still in there, hiding behind a stiff petal, or had he moved on to the shelf below? No, there was no web there, only a golden lighter with a symbol on it. Liana's eyes opened wider to make sure she wasn't seeing things. She wasn't; it was the same golden lighter with the Eshgh symbol that Taffi had used to roast crickets the night they spent together in the forest. Taffi had been there—and if she wasn't still so devastated by the events from the last couple of hours, she would have been ecstatic.

Liana got up and slowly moved toward it. Each step labored in the air for at least three seconds before completing its journey to the floor. She didn't know when Taffi came or what it meant, but she wanted to remain exact, controlled, and precise. She looked only at the lighter, as if trying to best it in a staring contest. Her eyes started to sting from the lack of natural lubricant waiting patiently in her eyelids. The image of the Eshgh on its side began to imprint on the lenses of Liana's eyes until it finally sank into her head. Could it be that all this time her ancestor was hidden in plain sight? Liana stepped back and braced herself.

"Accalia," she said.

There was nothing. Of course she wasn't hidden in plain sight; Stefan never would have risked losing her. Half disappointed and half relieved—for meeting your great ancestor who almost literally moved heaven and earth was a little intimidating—Liana grabbed the golden lighter off the shelf and stared down at it in her hand. The longer she looked, the more disappointed she became. No, it wouldn't be intimidating; it would be wonderful, thought Liana. She pressed down on the mechanism that created a spark and released the lighter fluid within, but there was no flame to follow. She did it again and again—still nothing. Not only was there no genie inside but no fuel either. It wasn't a devastating blow, but when the whole world has turned itself upside down, even a paper cut would be soul crushing. With nowhere else to direct her frustration, Liana slammed the lighter against her bed frame three times before she haphazardly jerked off its top. Dry cotton spilled out onto the floor. She sat on her bed and glared down at the sad thirsty lump. She wondered how long it had been in there, and why it was sparkling. *Sparkling?* With the indifference of a scorned teenager, Liana kicked the tiny sparkling wad of cotton across her bedroom floor and a tiny rock flew out. It skipped across a gap in the floorboards and settled just a few feet from the purple wall. Liana slid off of her bed and picked it up.

It was the painite gem that was on the locket in her dreams.

For the first time since she fastened my chains against her warm skin on the night of her father's first performance, I was taken off of Liana's ankle and placed carefully in the palm of her hand. There would be no more dreams—Liana knew what to do. I had prepared her for this and the rest of her half genie, half human life. Now it was my turn. Liana placed the gem in the flawed center of her locket and said once more: "Accalia."

There was no pomp and circumstance, no bells and whistles or over-the-top bravado that might accompany a younger genie. I stood before Liana as if standing in front of a mirror, our green eyes staring back at each other. I wanted to speak, to at least acknowledge her presence, but I couldn't. What do you say to a legend, to a vision, to the one thing that kept your heart beating for centuries? How I wished that I could have been free to nurture my bloodline from the beginning, only now to see that it has become stronger without me. Liana was more than a legend, she was beautiful yet beaten, flawless yet fractured, gentle yet fierce—she was everything.

I could feel her apprehension and only loved her more for it.

"You look just like my daughter," I said.

I reached out to touch Liana's cheek, and her eyes began to fill with tears. Too embarrassed to cry but too overcome to contain herself, Liana wrapped her arms around me and buried her face in my neck. Without warning, a culmination of pent-up energy, both bad and good, released inside our bodies. As it reached across us like a great tsunami flowing inland, our heads began to ache and our skin became flushed. For fear of seeming childish or naïve, Liana shut her eyes and pretended it wasn't happening.

"It's okay," I said, "you've been through a lot. More than most genies, half human or otherwise."

Liana lifted her head to reveal a smile. I smiled back, and before long we began to share a nervous laugh.

"So," I started, "what would you like to wish for?"

Liana had forgotten that she would be entitled to the

customary three wishes for releasing me from the locket. Although, ever since her dad's genie-themed show, she had often thought of what she would wish for if she had the chance. There was the typical want of money, power, and fame, but there was also an occasional desire for little things like non-frizzy hair on a humid day or odorless nail polish remover. Of course, now that she had the power to do almost everything, she didn't want much of anything…maybe just a couple of things, though, to save her the trouble of concentrating and all.

"I wish the house was clean," Liana said.

I smiled and winked my green eye. Before Liana knew what was happening, the house was impeccably clean. No more dust-covered picture frames, unmade beds, or dangling cobwebs; and it smelled better, too.

"What, no vomit?" said Liana as she recalled the Ghul method of granting wishes.

"No," I said, "I don't think I could cover the whole house."

We both smiled again and leaned into each other. As much fun as we were having, the next wish was a bit more serious.

"I wish my father to be released and have no memory of my disappearance," said Liana.

I knew Jamison was dear to Liana, so I granted the technically two wishes as one.

"It is done. And for your last wish?"

Liana peeked at me suspiciously.

"What do you mean?" she said. "That was three."

"Not on my count," I said.

Liana had played enough mind games in the last week to know what I was getting at. Of course, she didn't want to talk about it, not then, not yet.

"I don't want anything else," said Liana.

As I knew what Liana's response would be even before she responded, I had started to usher her over to the bed for a motherly talk. We both sat, trying not to disturb the military creases in the bed sheets, and leaned into each other's arms.

"I can bring him back," I said, "but only as a shell, like a human. His powers must remain with Stefan to keep him bonded."

Liana sat silently on the bed and stared at the floor where the jar of change had broken. Doubt crept in an out of her head like ants in and out of their tunneled homes. What if he's different? What if he leaves? Maybe he was right; maybe he will betray me again.

"Why do you think you couldn't bind Stefan the first time you tried?" I said.

"I don't know," said Liana.

"Only rage can move mountains," I said.

"But only forgiveness can bring them back together," said

Amon.

Liana stood up in shock.

"Amon!"

"It was your forgiveness for Taffi that gave you the power you needed, not rage," said Amon.

Amon and I looked at each other with the longing of a hundred orphans.

"My father may be hardheaded, but he is very wise," I said.

We fell into each other's arms for a reunion that was centuries in the making, and, like my release from the locket, there were no fireworks or dazzling displays of cosmic powers, only the love of a father and daughter, and our forgiveness for each other.

Liana had heard all the right things, had our blessing, and indeed wanted to wish for Taffi but still couldn't bring herself to do it. *Why? What was holding her back? Was it fear?* Again, doubt swarmed over any positive thoughts that tried to reach the surface of her mind, so much so that she even began to doubt our judgment of the situation.

"I know what it will be like for him," I said, "living a hundred years thinking of only one thing. There is no pain that can match it, not the pain of conditional love, or even the pain of betrayal."

I moved toward Liana and took her hand.

"You are a Marid, Liana. We do not run from our fears; we

face them. My prison kept me from my true love; don't let yours do the same."

Liana smiled, "True love?"

I smiled back and winked at her. The swarm in Liana's mind began to dissipate, and she stood confidently between Amon and me. She was indeed a Marid and, more than that, a powerful woman to be reckoned with. Liana looked at me and winked back. She carefully took the lamp that was now Stefan's prison out from the loose fabric of her garment and handed it to me.

"Please bring Taffi back to me," she said.

I handed the lamp to my father and smiled.

"As you wish."

Chapter 39

REBIRTH

They liked Japanese food. A plate of sashimi and roasted crickets sat in the middle of a bare hardwood floor. There was no soy sauce, rice, or wasabi—that would ruin the nostalgia. The plate, or rather the lid of a gallon-sized paint can, was clean but for the color label, now buried underneath a slab of Jell-O-like tuna. Removed for the first time, there was just one small dent in the lid's outer rim. Its counterpart sat on a large transparent tarp covering the other half of the empty room. There was just one can, a paint tray, and two brand new roller brushes. *I guess I was the third wheel.* Liana and Taffi, or Taff as we now called him, sat on the ground in front of me. I had only come to check on their progress, which was so far nonexistent. Liana had returned to her human garb, sporting cutoff jean shorts, flip-flops, and a paint-stained sweatshirt, while Taff wore a Green Bay Packers jersey, number four, and baggy mesh shorts. Even I had decided to try human clothes again—fashion had improved tremendously since the eighteenth century. I tried not to be too gaudy and had just put on a Tahari summer dress, heels, diamond earrings from Tiffany's and a Gucci clutch. *I didn't really need the clutch; it just seemed like the thing to do.*

The room was Jamison's old office, now cleared out to make room for their new edition. Taff had no money or family, so Jamison agreed to take him in—his old office was the furthest room from Liana's on the other side of the second floor. It clearly needed a new coat of paint, as the footprints from Jamison's posters spotted the walls like a stretch of dough that had just been pillaged by cookie cutters.

Liana picked up a piece of the tuna sashimi and extended it out toward Taff's mouth.

"I love the color you chose," I said, "it suits you."

Taff quickly turned his head in my direction, and the slimy block of raw fish grazed his cheek. Liana laughed, and Taff smiled as he transferred the slime from his cheek to his wrist.

"Yes, ma'am, I think so, too," said Taff.

"Please, call me Dahlia."

"Yes, Miss Dahlia."

I wasn't quite sure what he thought of me. He knew I could read his mind, so he would always think of sand when I was around—one continuous stream of free-falling sand, like in an hourglass. I could have pushed through and penetrated his true feelings, but I didn't, not yet. His new form and the world it inhabited would take some getting used to. He deserved his privacy. After all, he did not ask for this. I did feel, though, intermingled within the gains of falling sand, his love for Liana. It was real, and that was all that mattered.

"Are you going to stay and help us paint?" said Liana. *I knew she was being polite.*

"No, I just came by to say hello and check on your father."

"Okay, he's in the kitchen dipping the rest of the crickets in melted chocolate," said Liana.

"Sweet and salty, that's how I like them, too," I said.

Liana and Taff got up to see me out and then walked over to the can of paint waiting patiently on the protected floor. The corner of Taff's mouth spread out into a teasing grin.

"I think it does suit me," he said.

"Not me," said Liana, "I hate it."

She smiled, picked up the can, and poured purple paint into the tray.